DRUNK
ON THE
MOON

A ROMAN DALTON ANTHOLOGY

Edited by
PAUL D. BRAZILL

DARK VALENTINE PRESS

DARK VALENTINE PRESS
Cover and interior design by Indie Author Services

ISBN: 978-0-6156415-0-8

Dalton—he's his own "Death Squad" in ridding the world of those who don't contribute to the common good by his choice of victims when in his werewolf state, and Stateham also creates the element of sex, always a good thing in a story. Stateham delivers one image I wasn't expecting of Dalton—he's a quiche eater...I'm still trying to reconcile that with his werewolf/tough cop persona...

The next story up, "It's a Curse" by K.A. Laity, is a writer's delight. Like Brazill, Laity knocks your socks off with the language and also with the dialog. She also delivers a sex scene that leaves the reader alternately grimacing in pain and fantasizing about rough sex. Really rough sex... It's the dialog that grabs you more than anything. Brilliant.

John Donald Carlucci enters next with his take on Dalton in a tale titled "Silver Tears." Carlucci gets my nod for the best opening sentence of any of the stories, beginning with: "'Jesus, I think I stepped on an ear,' I said after nearly slipping and falling as I entered the taped-off crime scene." It instantly transported me into the story and I wasn't disappointed. You won't be, either. Not to give away the story, but it involves a pervert that wants Dalton to bite him so he can become a werewolf, and Dalton accommodates him...but with a twist. You don't want to miss the twist!

Julia Madeleine, with her offering "Fear the Night," gets Dalton out of England and over to Quebec, Canada, where he has a go with zombie strippers. If anyone doubts the veracity of zombie strippers, don't. I've been to Quebec and it's true.

Jason Michel weighs in with "Back to Nature," where Dalton takes a vacation in the woods with his friend Duffy the bartender. This was a delightful experience and the best way I can describe it is it's a stream-of-conscious cinematic experience that reads like poetry.

And then... Richard Godwin with his version of Roman

Dalton the werewolf he's titled, "Getting High on Daisy." All I can say about this one is this. WOW. This one was my favourite. Just brilliant writing. Every writer in this collection is the very best of writers working today. But Godwin went somewhere else with this one. A place very few of us are ever privileged to reach. This one was Jungian in the best sense as in the night dream level of story-telling. This one by itself is worth the price of the entire collection.

And, just when I thought nothing could match Godwin's story, I ran smack into Katherine Tomlinson's "A Fire in the Blood." Here's what I have to say about her tale. Read it. I wasn't familiar with her work before, but this story convinced me to run out and buy every word of hers that's for sale. It's that frickin' good! Good writing should provide surprises, and believe me—this one did! On every page. Before I read "A Fire in the Blood" I'd conferred the title of "best story in the collection" to Godwin. This one doesn't supplant his, but it's the co-winner, IMHO.

And then we come to the finale, Brazill's "Before the Moon Falls," his prequel to the collection. Brilliant. Just like the collection itself. I cannot remember a more consistently great collection of stories like this. *Drunk on the Moon* is going to end up on a lot of "Best of" lists at the end of the year. An awful lot of those lists…. It's already on mine.

Once you read it, I wager it'll be on yours…

—Les Edgerton, author of *The Bitch, Just Like That* and others

CONTENTS

INTRODUCTION

PAUL D. BRAZILL

ROMAN DALTON, your common or garden-variety werewolf private eye, first howled for the people behind Dark Valentine Press more than two years ago, and now he's prowled back into their lair!

This is how it happened.

A few years ago, there was a buzz across the internet about *Dark Valentine* magazine, a cool and beautifully designed pulp mag that would feature horror, noir, fantasy—stories of all genres—as well as cross-genre stories. I knew of some of the people involved and thought that this would be a pretty classy joint indeed.

And I wanted in.

And this is where the confluence comes in.

For a while, I'd been thinking that the Tom Waits' song "Drunk on the Moon" would make a great title for a werewolf story—Tom Waits was in the film *Wolfen*, and his gravelly voice could easily be that of a werewolf.

And then I thought that, maybe I could raise the stakes even higher and write a werewolf noir...

Hmmmm.

So I wrote "Drunk on the Moon," the story of a cop called Roman Dalton who works in the shadowy corners of a place known only as The City, and I sent it to *Dark Valentine* magazine. The story was accepted and published in the debut issue. It proved to be popular, too. I wrote another Roman Dalton story too and that was also accepted. And was also popular.

I went from chuffed to double chuffed. Indeed, I then had the great idea of sending lots of Roman Dalton stories to *Dark Valentine* magazine, but unfortunately it folded.

And then, somewhere along the way, I started reading The Dead Man, the fantastic series of books that Lee Goldberg and William Rabkin produced, written by a veritable cornucopia of pulp masters. I really liked their idea of different writers taking on the same character, I really did.

Roman Dalton's world was, I thought, full of possibilities, and I wondered if some of my favourite dark fiction writers would like to dip a toe into that world. So I asked. And most of them said yes.

Some of those stories were published elsewhere last year, but that didn't work out, and so it only seems fitting that Roman Dalton should return home.

So, here you have a "same world" anthology written by an international collection of dark fiction writers. Crime writers. Horror writers.

Here's who you have:

Paul D. Brazill (UK/Poland)
Allan Leverone (USA)
K.A. Laity (USA/Ireland)

B.R. Stateham (USA)
Julia Madeleine (Canada)
Richard Godwin (UK)
John Donald Carlucci (USA)
Frank Duffy (UK/Poland)
Jason Michel (UK/France)
Katherine Tomlinson (USA)

When a full moon fills the night sky, private investigator Roman Dalton becomes a werewolf and prowls The City's neon and blood-soaked streets.

—*Paul D. Brazill*

DRUNK ON THE MOON

PAUL D. BRAZILL

IT'S HAPPENED TO MOST PEOPLE at one time or another. Maybe after a birthday party or a fight with the wife.

You wake up throbbing with gloom and aching with guilt. Memories of the previous night trample all over your thoughts with dirty feet. Nausea curdles away inside you. Your mouth's like the bottom of a bird cage and Keith Moon is playing a drum solo in your head. You peel back your eyelids and shards of sunlight slice through the blinds. Your bedroom looks as if it's been redecorated by winos.

You stagger to your feet and stumble into the migraine-bright bathroom to puke. You're sweating, shaking, and pins and needles acupuncture your body. Your clothes are torn and covered in blood. And then the waves of dark memories come flooding back like a tsunami.

Like I say, it happens to most people every now and again. But to me it happens with regularity every month. Three times a month, to be precise.

And it happened again last night.

The oil slick of night was melting into a granite grey day and dark, malignant clouds were spreading themselves across the morning sky as a battered yellow taxi with blacked-out windows spluttered to a halt in front of my apartment block.

I pushed past an overdressed Russian woman, who struggled to control a black umbrella that fluttered and flapped like a big black bat trying to escape from her grip. Ignoring her protests, I grabbed the handle and opened the door.

I shuffled into the back seat of the cab as Duffy, the driver, blew his nose on a Santa Claus napkin and threw it out of the window. Duffy's face was so acne-scarred it looked like a chewed up toffee apple, and his spidery quiff was dyed black as ink. Not what you'd call a sight for sore eyes, then.

"Shitty, morning, eh, Roman?" said Duffy.

"I've had better," I said, slumping against the car door.

Duffy hummed along to Mel Tormé's "Gloomy Sunday," struck a match on the "No Smoking" sign and lit up a Cuban cigar.

"The Velvet Fog," said Duffy, raising his bushy eyebrows. I said nothing. "His nickname used to be the Velvet Fog."

I ignored him and stared out of the window as he started up the car and ran a red light. At this time of day the streets were littered with the dregs of society. Bottom-feeders. Lowlifes.

"Twilight time," Duffy said, his face sweating even though the air inside the cab was as cold as the grave.

"That's what we used to call this time of day, twilight time. You know, like the song?"

And then he was silent again, apart from his teeth grinding and the clicking sound that his jaw made.

The taxi snaked its way along the sea front, past pubs, greasy spoons, sex shops, and kebab shops before stuttering to a full stop outside Duffy's Bar. The rain fell down in sheets and the fading streetlights shimmered, reflected in the taxi's windscreen.

Duffy got out, pulled up the metal shutters, and opened up the bar.

As Duffy switched on the lights, the jukebox burst to life. Howlin' Wolf snarled out "I Ain't Superstitious" as I nestled on my usual bar stool, calmly contemplating the double whisky that Duffy had placed in front of me. The ice cubes seemed to shimmer, glimmer, and glow in the wan light. Twilight time, indeed.

I briefly turned my gaze outside. The wet pavement reflected Duffy's Bar's flickering neon sign. A gangling scarecrow rushed past the window and burst through the door.

Tall and with long black hair, Detective Ivan Walker flew in out of the storm like a murder of crows, bringing rain and a waft of golden leaves behind him. He wore a tattered long black raincoat that flapped in the breeze.

He took the stool next to me and put his badge and his Colt Anaconda on the bar. Duffy poured him a death-black espresso.

"Twilight time again, Roman," rasped Walker in a voice like broken glass.

"So I heard," I said.

Howlin' Wolf ended and was replaced by Dusty Springfield.

"The White Negress," said Duffy, looking up from his *National Geographic*. "That was her nickname. It wasn't racist, though."

He was a mine of information, he really was.

I took in Walker's appearance. His face — almost angelic — was latticed with scars. On the side of his neck was a burn mark shaped like a pentangle.

My hands were shaking, and I slurped my whisky with all the enthusiasm of an ex-con in a bordello.

"Hair of the dog that bit you?" said Walker, as I poured myself another drink.

I said nothing. It was a tired old line but not as tired as I felt. But then, two nights on the prowl will do that to you.

"Tough couple of days, then?" said Walker.

I shrugged.

"It's a dog's life, eh?" he said.

I ignored him, closed my eyes, and let the booze wash over me.

"Did you boys hear about the murders last night?" said Walker, stretching his arms and yawning.

"Can't say I did," said Duffy.

"Really?" said Walker. "It's been all over the news."

"Don't follow the news," said Duffy. "Depressing."

"Oh, this is a good one, though. A couple of Ton Ton Philippe's boys were sliced up and ripped to pieces outside The Pink Pussy Club."

Duffy and I ignored him, but I knew Walker well enough to know that he wasn't just here to chat.

"And?" I said, eyes still closed.

"Oh, no great loss to the world. Don't get me wrong, these boys were scum. They work for that Haitian lunatic, for fuck's sake. I mean, good riddance to them and a round of applause to whoever did it. Yeah, but we've not much to go on, although, it looks to me like they were ripped apart by a pack of dogs. Maybe the even same ones that took out Ice-Pick Mick McKinley last month."

"Ah."

"But…" I heard him shuffle in his pocket. "We did get one possible lead. We found this in the remains of one of the chewed-up hands that had been severed and hurled across the alley."

I heard the metal scrape across the top of the bar and I knew what it was.

I opened my eyes.

Next to my whisky was a blood-splattered badge. My detective's badge.

"Let's be careful out there, Officer Dalton," said Walker as he knocked back the coffee, patted me on the back, and headed out of the bar.

"Bollocks," said Duffy, drinking vodka straight from the bottle. "Ton Ton Philippe!" He shook his head. "You're playing with the big boys now, Roman."

As the White Negress sang "I Close My Eyes and Count to Ten," I did the very same thing. Only, I made it up to one hundred.

The City's brilliant neon cast dense shadows that tried to mask its sordid secrets, but a stench still permeated the alleyways and the gutters and the bars. Of course, the stink overpowered some people, smothered them. But not me. I just took a deep breath and breathed in. Inhaled it deeply.

I'd worked as a cop in the city for twenty years: robbery, vice, homicide. But that all changed when I stumbled into what sounded like a typical drunken bar brawl and I ended up in something far, far from typical.

It was way past midnight and a full moon grasped the sky. I sat half-asleep in my car outside The Playhouse at the bottom of Banks' Hill. I was on a stake-out looking out for Ice-Pick Mick McKinley, a rat-faced coke fiend who had told me that he had a wad of information on Ton Ton Philippe, the Haitian gangster whose control of The City was spreading like a cancer.

Suddenly, a sickly stew of screams and howls clung to the wind and drifted down to my car.

The moonlight oozed across The City's dank cobblestones like quicksilver, creeping between the cracks, crawling into the gutters. I got out of the car and slowly walked up the hill, my breath appearing in front of me like a specter.

As I got closer to Duffy's Bar, I shivered, pulled my long black overcoat close to me, and carefully pushed open the large oak door. Checking my pistol, I stepped into the bar.

The room was suffocating in red velvet and leather. Chandeliers hung from a mirrored ceiling, and half-eaten corpses littered the concrete floor. And around them, feasting, were some sort of creatures—half-man, half-wolf.

Instinctively, I fired off a round of bullets, but the creatures didn't flinch. They just crawled towards me, snarling and growling.

Then I noticed Duffy on top of the oak bar, lighting a rag that he'd stuffed in a bottle of booze. He threw it at a jukebox near the creatures and it exploded like a volcano.

The next few moments were a flash of fireworks and explosions. As the smoke subsided, the wolf creatures were in front of me. And then they pounced.

I awoke in an antiseptic-stinking hospital, with Walker beside me eating grapes and playing Sudoku. He told me that after the explosion one of Duffy's silver chandeliers had crashed down on my attackers, who had somehow struggled from under it and crawled away.

The corpses of three half-naked bikers were found in an alleyway by Walker and his boys the next morning. Long-haired, bearded weirdoes, he said. From out of town. Me? Well, they said I was lucky to be alive. Ravaged, was the word they used. I was given long-term sick leave to recover.

And so I embraced my sick leave as well as most chronic workaholic cops and filled my days and nights watching reality television, eating junk food, and getting wasted on cheap whisky.

Until the end of the month that is, when a full moon filled the autumn night like a big silver dollar. And then? Well, then, I just got drunk on the moon.

Days bled into weeks, which hemorrhaged into months, until the winter crept up and smothered the whiskey-coloured autumn days with darkness. Night after night, Duffy's flickering neon sign dragged me back like an umbilical cord. Or maybe a noose.

It was early one Sunday evening, the next full moon was a week away, and Duffy's was half full. The Wurlitzer jukebox played an old Johnny Layton song and I was in my pots, watching a spectral spiral of smoke drift up from the ashtray towards the big silver star that hung above the bar all year 'round.

It dangled, slightly askew, just to the left of the spiderweb-cracked clock. Its tinsel border had pretty much molted to almost nothing, and the glittery red "Merry Xmas" greeting had dandruffed so many barflies over the years that it was almost unreadable.

A gust of wind blew the door open, and Duffy retreated to the shadows. Outside, a sharp sliver of moon garrotted the coal-black sky. A tall woman, her long hair as black as a raven's wings, drifted across the road, oblivious to the mob of traffic. Duffy licked his lips, and his eyes glittered and glowed with each car's near miss.

Almost as if on cue, the night was suddenly filled with the crackle of exploding fireworks, and Daria oozed into the bar like mercury. She stood before me looking like a long drink of water crying out to a thirsty man and a chill sliced through me like a stiletto. Her eyes glowed bright emerald green and then faded to black as she smiled, a slash of red lipstick across her full lips.

"Detective Dalton," she said, in a voice as dark and thick as the smoke from a French cigarette.

"That's ex-Detective Dalton," I slurred. "I'm retired now. A full-fledged member of the self-employed community." The words tripped over themselves as they tumbled out of my mouth.

I handed Daria a business card. I had hundreds of them. Since Duffy convinced me to become a private eye, I'd had the grand total of one client.

"Can I get you a drink?" I asked.

"The night is young, Detective Dalton," she said as she walked through the Ace of Spades archway and stepped upon a small chiaroscuro-lit stage. "Even if you are not!"

She chuckled as two massive, bald men with bullet-hole eyes appeared out of the shadows and helped her with her long black raincoat. They moved a drum kit, a double bass, and an old RKO Radio microphone onto the stage as Daria languorously smoked a black cigarette.

I turned back toward Duffy, his head in a worn copy of *National Geographic*.

"How was last night?" I asked.

"The fancy dress party wasn't exactly a flop," said Duffy, without looking up from his magazine. "It was just that everyone came as a table and chairs."

I smiled weakly, tried to think of a witty reply, gave up, and lit another cigarette.

"Another JD?" asked Duffy

I shrugged and nodded at the same time. No mean feat, the state I was in. He poured me another drink and pulled the plug on the jukebox. I turned towards the stage as Daria's laugh filled the room. And then she started to sing.

The sweat trickled down the back of my neck like an insect as the drumsticks scuttled across the drums and the bass player's fingers snaked down the fret board. I shivered as Daria whispered a torch song, as if it was her dying breath and sparked the embers of a dream.

I quickly downed my drink, ordered another one and headed toward oblivion like dishwater down a plughole.

The winter moon hung fat and gibbous as I tore Long Tom Short's head from his shoulders and hurled it across the snow-smothered ground. The splashes of blood looked black in the stark moonlight. A murder of crows scattered and sliced through the whiteness, as the purr of an approaching Mercedes grew to a roar and melded with my howls.

The car screeched to a stop in a nearby alleyway, outside the former church that had been converted into The Pink Pussy night-club. The driver got out, holding a Colt Anaconda. Dressed in the long black overcoat, and wearing a wide-brimmed hat, he looked like a shadow as he cut through the deserted car park. I growled as he approached, struggling, as always, to control my wolf-self.

"Down, Rover," said Detective Ivan Walker, my former part-ner, as he looked around at the six or seven dead bodies spread around the car park.

"You have been a busy boy tonight, Dalton," he said, his voice like sandpaper. "Ton Ton Philippe is gonna have to recruit a new crew if you keep wasting his boys like this. Either that or corpse you." He scratched the pentangle-shaped scar on his neck with the barrel of his gun.

Snow began to fall like confetti. Walker took Long Tom by the ankles and hauled the gargoyle's massive corpse towards the dark and dingy alley, leaving a snaking trail of blood behind him. I sniffed the smell of death and my heart beat like a drum.

Walker pulled Long Tom Short up to the car, illuminated by the light from a stained glass window, and opened the boot. He hauled the cadaver inside and slammed the lid shut.

I could almost taste the warm flesh. The red splashes were spreading like a Rorschach test before my eyes. The bloodlust was no longer possible to control. I leapt toward Walker and gave a cavernous roar as he dropped to his knees, pointed the gun, and fired it straight into my heart.

I slammed into the back of the car and crumpled to the ground. Walker rose to his feet and stood over me, smoking a cigar, the smoke rings floating above his head like a halo or a crown of thorns. Behind him I saw the shape of a tall, dark-haired woman in the corner of the alleyway. Her eyes glowed emerald green and then faded to black.

And then the sea of sleep engulfed me.

Dark dreams lapped at the shore of my sleep until I awoke drowning in sweat. I adjusted my eyes. The digital clock beside my bed said that it was midday. I was naked on my bed, the black sheets ripped to shreds, and I was dashed with cuts and bruises.

Above my heart were three small punctures. Walker was a crack shot and the darts, filled with traces of silver, were just enough to knock me out for the count without actually killing me.

I showered and dressed in black jeans and a black roll-neck sweater. It was cold and I sat at the Formica table near the rasping radiator, sipping strong black coffee and nibbling on a piece of burnt toast. I clicked on my Bakelite radio and listened to a George Jones song while I tried to read To Have and Have Not. It was no good. Once again, my concentration was shot to pieces. I pulled on my Doc Martin boots, picked up my overcoat, and headed off to Duffy's.

The thing is, I didn't particularly care whether she was lying to me or telling me the truth, since most of what I'd told her had been dug up from some murky hinterland somewhere on the outskirts of honesty.

It was like a hunt, and it didn't seem to matter who the hunter was and who was the game.

"So, will you do it?" asked Daria, sipping her glass of absinthe. She leaned close to me so she could hear my reply. The Frog Boys were slamming coins into the jukebox, playing '70s punk. I was in no condition to tell them to change their tune. The Frog Boys weren't the understanding type.

If Ton Ton Phillipe had one rival in The City, then Count Otto Rhino was that man. The Frog Boys were Rhino's seemingly invincible front line troops. All of them were well over six feet tall, with arms like tree trunks, and dressed in military fatigues.

"Well?" said Daria. Her perfume was a poison that I couldn't get enough of. I shrugged, knowing full well that I would do as she asked.

A glass shattered in the corner of the room. I ignored it.

"Oh, yeah," I said "I'll just turn up at The Pink Pussy and grab your kid sister out of there. I'm sure Ton Ton Philippe won't mind. I mean, Haitian voodoo priests are renowned for their easygoing manner. Especially the ones that run most of The City's underworld."

She grinned.

"And don't forget his army of zombie henchmen," she said, her eyes flashing crimson.

"Oh, yeah. Mustn't forget them."

"So? You're in?"

"It'll cost you."

"Oh, I can pay, detective. I'm good for it."

"Then I'm in," I said. "Like Errol Flynn."

Daria leaned back in her bar stool and smiled. "Another round of drinks," she said to Duffy.

Duffy picked up a bottle of absinthe and placed it on the bar. Suddenly, the bar stool shook. Two or three of The Frog Boys were slam-dancing and singing—well, screaming—about being Cranked Up Really High. And they surely were. Just as Duffy poured our drinks, one of the behemoths splayed into me, spilling the violent green liquid across the bar.

"Asshole!" I yelled, without thinking.

"What did you call me?" asked the giant.

Before I could answer, he had me by the throat with one gigantic paw and was wrenching me off the bar stool with ease.

I was helpless. I could see Duffy's fingers creeping towards the shotgun that was hidden under the bar, but before he could get near it, the jukebox stopped and there was silence. Then, the wisp of a melody. It was soft, but it slowly grew louder. Daria was singing and patting the giant on his arm. Her eyes glowing green.

"No, Duke," she said.

Suddenly, he started to sob and dropped me back in my seat. Daria stroked his cheek. "Go play nice, Duke," she said.

"Yes, Miss Daria," said the sniffling Duke. "Sorry."

And he walked back to the rest of The Frog Boys, who all sat around the table, heads in hands. The jukebox clicked back to life. Miles Davis played warm melody. And no one complained.

The Pink Pussy was usually crammed full of the sort of people that give pond life a bad name. Politicians, senior police officers, lawyers, actors. The DJ, Fritz Neuman, was a gaunt, pallid man who looked as if he's been dead for a decade and no one had bothered to tell him. Each night he played something with a pounding, deafening bass. The dance floor would be cramped with hot and sweaty bodies. On the stage, partially clad young women slid around like spaghetti on an alcoholic's plate.

But in the afternoons the place was half empty. The flotsam and jetsam of life were scattered around the place, drinking, sleeping. I almost felt at home.

I sat at the bar and glanced at my watch. Like with so many things, the secret of tonight's success would be timing.

"Drink?" said the tattooed greaser behind the bar.

"Bourbon," I said.

I picked up my drink and headed toward a darkened corner. Toward Ton Ton Philippe.

Small, with a mohawk and an eye patch, Philippe sat on a golden throne near the stage. Snakes twisted around his arms, hissing violently. A teenage girl was curled up in his lap like a Persian kitten.

"Detective Dalton," he said, nodding. I didn't correct him.

"What can I do for you?"

"Her," I said, nodding toward the squirming little blond.

"Ah, I'm afraid this little fresh piece of chicken is reserved for a special customer. And what the Lao want, the Lao get."

There was a beat as we locked eyes, and then I whipped out my gun.

"I'm not buying," I said. "I'm taking." And I pulled her towards me.

Philippe's laugh echoed around the place. And then they appeared. Three of them. Behemoths. Torn and ragged flesh. Glassy eyes. Zombies? Maybe? It certainly seemed as if the rumors were true. But before I could contemplate this any further, they stepped toward me and I fell into a well of blackness.

Ton Ton Philippe's office was warm. Stiflingly so. I was strapped to a metal chair, like an insect trapped in amber. A parrot screeched in the corner of the room.

"Now, what do we do with you?" said Philippe. "I think that eradicating an officer of the law may give me more problems than I need but…"

I was barely listening to him. I could feel the itch crawling across my flesh. It wouldn't be long now. Outside the window, a milky moon filled the inky sky. I changed.

It was a blur of crimson. Of howls and screams.

The zombies were soon ripped to shreds, but Ton Ton Philippe was gone in a wisp of smoke. The girl was like a rag doll as I picked her up and smashed through the window into the bitter cold night air.

"Thanks, Detective," said Daria. "You did a damned good job." We sat at a rickety table in a deserted Duffy's. She had the blonde on her knee, and I saw that they didn't look a lot like sisters. Or kiss like sisters, either. I'd been taken for a ride. A one-way ticket on a runaway train. My flesh prickled. My bones ached. I didn't even care.

Daria stood, The Frog Boys beside her. "Back home to Daddy, sweetie," she said to the blonde, who stumbled to her feet, a smirk on her face. They headed outside and got into a dark green stretch limo with a crest on the side. The crest of Count Otto Rhino.

I looked down at the cash-filled envelope that Daria had given me. Stuffed with more green leaves than you'd find in a cabbage patch. I'd made some money. And an enemy of Ton Ton Philippe. Not a bad night's work, all in all.

"JD?" said Duffy, tearing up a beer mat.

"Naw, I need a kiss from *la fée verte*."

"Huh?" said Duffy.

"The Green Fairy. Give me a shot of absinthe," I said as I walked toward the bar. "I've heard it makes the heart grow fonder."

Paul D. Brazill is the creator of the *Drunk on the Moon* series. He was born in England and now lives in Poland. He has had writing published in various magazines and anthologies, including *The Mammoth Book of Best British Crime 8*. He's also had two collections published: *13 Shots of Noir* and *Snapshots*. His novella *Guns of Brixton* will be published in spring 2012. His blog is "You Would Say That, Wouldn't You?"

THE DARKE AFFAIR

ALLAN LEVERONE

THE CLOUDS RACED THROUGH THE SKY seemingly just above my head, the full moon's leering face appearing through the grey-black curtain hanging above The City for a scant second or two every few minutes before again disappearing. But I knew it was there. Oh, yes, I knew. And now, so did another group of Ton Ton Philippe's boys.

The breeze swirled, moving hot, fetid air around like a drunk staggering along a dark alley, trying to find his way home to puke and pass out, not necessarily in that order. Like me, most of the time, in other words.

But I wasn't drunk tonight, at least not on cheap whiskey. Tonight, a different liquid's siren song moved me, calling out to me as strongly as rotgut did the rest of the month. I smelled blood. I needed blood. And Philippe's crew was giving it, albeit unwillingly.

I had made a full-fledged enemy of the Haitian gangster by stealing a girl literally right off the fat fuck's lap. My torch-singer friend Daria had spun a sob story about the girl being her sister, and blah, blah, blah. It was, of course, all a lie, but what did I care? Daria had offered real money for the job and it wasn't like clients were knocking down the door of an alcoholic ex-cop PI with certain…physiological issues.

In any event, Ton Ton had sworn revenge, and while it had taken some time for him to try to collect, tonight was a pretty clear indication Philippe had not forgotten about me.

I ripped the head off one punk, a kid so young he didn't look old enough to buy a drink legally, not that he would have to worry about that now. The head was surprisingly heavy, like a misshapen bowling ball, and it was spurting blood and trailing veins, ligaments, and assorted other squishy, wet tissue. The kid's eyes rolled up into his head as his body dropped to the pavement with a wet plop, which was just as well. It prevented him from seeing what happened next.

I pitched the corpse-head into the face of the second of Philippe's boys, the two craniums whacking together like a bowl-ing alley strike. The second kid hit the ground before the first kid's head dropped next to him, and I advanced on him and slashed off a couple of important body parts, just to ensure he would never work for Ton Ton again. Assuming he lived, an assumption which seemed farfetched based on his injuries.

The third member of Philippe's crew took off running, prov-ing smarter than I would've given him credit for when he pulled a little .22 pistol from his pocket and started the festivities by fir-ing at me. And missing.

I stood over the two bodies, breathing heavily, not from exer-tion but from excitement and blood-lust. I was satisfied with the result of my evening's work but confused by the timing. Why the hell had Philippe sent his crew tonight, of all nights? Did he pay so little attention to the calendar and the phases of the moon that he was ignorant of the danger to his boys, or did he simply not care? Maybe there were factors at play I was missing, as my mind swirled with blotchy crimson images of death and destruction. Philippe certainly seemed to have no trouble replacing dead gang members, an ongoing testament to the sense of hopelessness and despair permeating The City, and especially its young men.

None of tonight's events made any sense, but then again, I wasn't about to lose any sleep over them. A couple of dead bloodthirsty murdering thugs—a couple more, that is—was no cause for concern, at least not on my part, and probably not on Detective Walker's, either.

And speaking of losing sleep, it occurred to me with the suddenness of a baseball bat to the side of the head that I was exhausted. I swayed where I stood. The energy it took to accomplish The Change was staggering; it was roughly comparable to running a marathon road race while juggling a chainsaw, a bowling pin, and a sleeping baby. That, combined with the effort I had expended dealing with Ton Ton Philippe's welcoming committee, had rendered me about as lively as a zombie. I almost wished there were some around; I would've fit right in.

I smiled at that ridiculous thought and began trudging toward the mouth of the alley and the road that would take me home. All I could think about was falling into bed and sleeping for about the next twenty-four hours.

Then that elusive moon shone through a break in the clouds, bathing the empty three a.m. streets and gutters of The City with a dirty glow. It was like looking through a window caked with a couple of decades' worth of grit and grime. And that was when I saw him. At least, I think it was a "him." Maybe it was an "it." A tall skeletal man in a long trench coat, fedora perched low on his head like a wooden ball atop a newel post, standing motionless next to a long black sedan. It was an old car, a really old one, so ancient that a car like it probably hadn't been seen in The City since my old man's old man roamed the streets.

I froze in mid-step. Although the stranger's face was covered in the shadows provided by his headwear and the predawn darkness, I knew the guy was looking directly at me. And the fight with Ton Ton's boys—if you could even call it a fight—had taken place at the end of the alleyway. Directly in the man's line of sight.

My first thought was, *Ivan Walker*. But it couldn't be the detective, because as tall and gangly as my ex-partner was, this mysterious fellow was even taller and skinnier. I wouldn't have thought it possible if I wasn't seeing it with my own eyes. Walker was about the thinnest living human being I had ever seen. Until now. This man was positively cadaverous.

I began inching forward. I wasn't sure how to respond to the stranger's unexpected appearance, but I suspected he might be another of Philippe's boys, maybe a second wave sent to finish off what his first group had so pathetically started. I wasn't worried, though. Even as exhausted as I was, I knew I possessed reserves of energy that would make my strength far superior to whatever this wasted piece of skin and bones could throw at me.

I took one step, then another, moving out of the mouth of the alley and toward the strange, long black car. Along with other handy abilities, the werewolf state allowed me to move with almost inconceivable speed when I chose to. Still, I knew I was too far away to catch the man by surprise. I had to get closer, and then I would make my move.

But almost as if the walking skeleton could read my thoughts, he began backing toward his open car door as I edged forward. It was a life-and-death dance, one being performed with balletic precision. A little farther and I would be close enough to strike.

Then the man raised his bare hand, extending his forefinger and folding his other three fingers into his palm before making a trigger out of his thumb. He pointed the make-believe pistol at me and squeezed the makeshift trigger and made a clicking noise with his tongue inside his cheek. It rang out like an actual gunshot to my sensitive ears, incredibly clear-sounding in the stillness of the City night, so much so that I flinched, turning my head and ducking.

The stranger chuckled—that was loud and clear, also—before sliding behind the wheel of his hearse-like vehicle and rumbling down the street, rolling toward me, then past. I was too stunned to move. I thought I could see him smiling as he drove by, but perhaps it was my imagination. Perhaps not.

Either way, by the time I recovered my wits sufficiently to give chase, the car, and the stranger driving it, had turned a corner and disappeared. I hesitated a moment, then loped toward my home.

Business was slow inside Duffy's Bar, a circumstance which suited me just fine. I was still exhausted from The Change and the run-in with Ton Ton's boys. Although I had spent two days recovering inside my apartment, I still felt like last week's chow mein leftovers and knew it would be another couple of days before I started feeling normal, which, for someone like me, has to be considered a relative term anyway.

But despite feeling like my insides had been scoured with steel wool and then rinsed with acid, I marched my sorry ass to Duffy's, where I currently sat soaking up the atmosphere. Or at least the JD. A couple of barflies who looked as though they had passed the age of consent during the Nixon administration hung around the Wurlitzer juke, playing pussy stuff, chick music that Duffy hated. I wondered why he didn't just pull the damned songs out of the machine—it was his bar, after all—but decided I didn't care enough to ask.

I was here for one reason. Besides the whiskey, that is. I drained my glass, and before the empty hit the table Duffy had replaced it with another. The guy may have been a lousy businessman but he was one hell of a perceptive bartender. I lifted the glass in tribute. It was dirty, but I wouldn't have expected otherwise.

"Walker been in lately?" I asked, and by way of response, Duffy glanced over my shoulder and lifted his chin. I turned and there was Ivan, tall and thin, black hair hanging listlessly almost to his shoulders. His strangely innocent-looking face, scarred but with a somehow almost angelic quality, was set and hard. He eased onto the stool next to me, the one that was never taken when I was in the house. People seemed nervous around me since becoming infected, without even knowing why.

I offered him a drink and he refused, as expected, choosing instead a cup of coffee, probably from the pot that had been brewed the last time Walker dropped by. Coffee wasn't the beverage of choice for most of Duffy's clientele. My friend took a sip and grimaced. "You heard about Ton Ton's boys." He said it as a statement, not a question. I didn't answer and he continued. "This messiness has to end, Roman. It's drawing the attention of the wrong people."

"Would one of those people be a skinny fuck who looks like Ichabod Crane with a head?"

Walker leveled his stony cop gaze at me, obviously trying to make me uncomfortable, conveniently forgetting I had employed the same tactic thousands of times over the decades we worked together before my "accident." If he was trying to intimidate me, it wasn't going to stand a snowball's chance in hell of working. Reluctantly, he smiled, his lips twisting into a thin bloodless slash that might have been more frightening than his stare. "You've met my new friend, then?" he asked.

"Not exactly." I wasn't sure how much to say, not wanting to put my ex-partner in more of a spot than he already was. "Let's just say we've never been properly introduced."

"Make sure it stays that way," Walker said, draining his coffee and placing the mug on the bar, watching a thin sludge that might have been coffee grounds gather in a toxic ooze at the bottom of the cup. "The guy's a Fed; he's here investigating all the shit that's been going on in The City. You want to stay under his radar. Trust me."

I said nothing, thinking, It might be too late for that, mate.

Walker stood and nodded at Duffy, who had been observing our conversation, if you could call it that, from the end of the bar. Duff was all squinty-eyed and serious, as if he could hear us, although at that distance it was impossible. Walker spun on his heel and clomped out the door, his raincoat flapping, the hot, dirty breeze pushing street trash into the bar in his wake.

Duffy shook his head in disgust, whether at Walker or at the trash I could not tell, and grabbed his broom to clear away the clutter.

There was nothing I could do about the Fed and what he may or may not have witnessed, so why would I worry? What's done is done, as the expression goes, and no amount of regret or recrimination is going to change it. Besides, maybe the guy hadn't really seen anything two nights ago as I was tearing Ton Ton's boys apart like a cheap shirt unraveling at the seams. I was probably whistling past the graveyard—the mysterious stranger had had a clear view directly down the alley as I was doing my thing—but maybe he had pulled up in that long black car after all the action had ended.

Maybe.

Regardless, worrying about it wasn't going to accomplish

anything, so I responded to Duffy's inquiring glance with a shrug, smiling in appreciation as he poured another drink. I wasn't against telling Duff everything, but what was there to tell?

The whiskey performed its duties as expected, cloaking the world in a misty alcoholic gauze, anesthetizing my body but making me feel even more tired than before. Maybe if I staggered to my apartment and fell into bed for another twelve hours or so, I would begin feeling like myself again by tomorrow. Hope springs eternal, right?

I paid Duff and walked out into the filthy City streets, wondering whether any more trash had blown into the bar as I exited, and whether even now poor Duffy was sweeping the detritus into a dustpan, shaking his head as he had done when Walker departed. The streets were mostly deserted, having been surrendered by the denizens of the day to the creatures of the night: the homeless drunks stumbling blindly through the bleak landscape, warming their hands over sewer grates releasing the stench of foul City air; the thugs skittering from darkened alleyway to darkened alleyway, preying on the weak and the unsuspecting; the sick and depraved, the dregs of society. And me.

I turned a corner and there he was. The Fed. The man from two nights ago who may or may not have witnessed me do the impossible. The man Walker had said to stay away from. He loomed in front of me, appearing out of nowhere, obviously having waited in the shadows of a crumbling, abandoned building for me to leave Duffy's.

I stumbled back, startled. Up close the man looked even more emaciated than he had at a distance. I wouldn't have thought it possible. His face was drawn and sunken, as if trying to consume itself, and his Adam's apple bobbed grotesquely when he swallowed. A fedora covered his scalp just as it had done two nights ago, and his trench coat flapped in the stifling City breeze exactly as Walker's had leaving Duffy's Bar. The long black car was nowhere to be seen.

"Roman Dalton, I presume?" he said, parting a pair of cracked lips to reveal a mouthful of tiny yellow teeth.

I tried to recover my bearings, not wanting to show how badly I had been startled. The whiskey had made my reactions slow, ponderous. "Who wants to know?"

"Agent Darke." The stick-figure of a man flashed an open wallet in my face, then flipped it closed as quickly as it had been produced. Presumably he had been offering his identification, although a speed-reader wouldn't have been able to inspect the shield, even if there was enough light to read it, which there wasn't. Streetlights weren't a priority in The City's municipal budget and hadn't been for a long, long time.

"Darke?"

"That's right."

"Do you have a first name?"

He smiled. "Agent," he said.

I tried to brush past him. He reached out and clutched my shoulder with one bony hand. His touch felt skeletal but deceptively strong. I glared at him and he lowered his hand. I took that as a small victory. "I know," he hissed.

"Is that so? What exactly is it you think you know?"

"Enough," he answered, his voice low and sibilant, exactly what you might expect from a snake. "And what I don't know I'll figure out. Things are happening in The City that the government would like to learn more about."

"I don't know what you're talking about."

"Please, Mr. Dalton, do not embarrass yourself. Surely a P.I. cannot procure clients without a modicum of intelligence."

I thought about telling him I hadn't actually "procured" a client in quite some time, that my business had been as dry as a ninety-year-old nun in the Sahara, but instead kept my mouth shut. I've been on the other side of this type of conversation plenty of times, and rarely does anything good come from the suspect talking. About anything. Especially after a night of drinking.

Agent Darke looked me up and down, and I wondered what he saw as a smile flickered across his ghastly face and disappeared. Then he whispered, "We'll talk again," and he stepped back, bowing with a flourish as he allowed me to pass. I edged along the littered sidewalk until Darke was behind me, then continued through the dark City streets toward my apartment, wondering what in the hell had just happened.

When I turned to look behind me he was gone.

Three weeks later

"We need to talk." Walker plopped himself down on the always available stool next to me at Duffy's and stared at me gravely.

I grabbed a stale pretzel from a grimy bowl and plopped it into my mouth. It wasn't much of a dinner, but the price was right. If I didn't pick up a paying client soon, I would be eating every meal at Duffy's. Or drinking it. I regarded my former partner; he looked even more unhealthy than usual, his face a deathly pallor broken only by dark circles under his eyes exactly the shade of the sky before a thunderstorm.

"Who died?" I cracked, expecting a laugh or at least a smile. I got neither.

"Have you seen Agent Darke recently?" he asked without preamble, the question catching me by surprise.

"I talked to him a few weeks ago," I said. "The creepy son of a bitch accosted me on the way home from Duffy's, asking all sorts of strange questions and making vague threats. After that, I saw him around for a while, always in unusual places and at unusual times."

"What was he doing?"

"Watching me, I assumed. I haven't seen him for a few days, though. Guess he got bored and moved on."

"Guess again," Walker said, biting down on a pretzel and wincing like he had just taken a bite of dog shit. He spit the food into his hands and looked around, finally shrugging and dumping the mess onto the floor. Duffy wouldn't be happy when he saw it. "Darke hasn't left The City at all. I got a tip from one of Count Otto Rhino's boys that Ton Ton Philippe grabbed Darke's ass. That means it's only a matter of time before Philippe ices him, if he hasn't already done so."

"What possible reason would Ton Ton have to do that? Darke's here because of me, not Ton Ton Philippe."

"You know that and I know that, but Ton Ton doesn't know that. He found out the Feds were sniffing around and assumed he was the focus of their investigation."

I nodded. "Makes sense. Ton Ton's into some nasty shit."

Walker stared at me and I knew he was waiting for me to say something, but for the life of me I couldn't imagine what it might be. Bobby Darrin's voice floated across the bar, singing about Mack the Knife and a body oozin' life.

Finally I couldn't take it anymore. I spread my hands. "What?"

"What do you mean 'what'? We have to do something about it."

"Why? This seems like the perfect solution to the Darke problem. Takes the focus off me. If one malnourished federal agent has to disappear, too fucking bad. It's not my problem."

"It will be, you stupid bastard. Christ, have you gotten dumber since being infected? Who was Darke focused on?"

"Me."

"And who do you think Darke's superiors are going to focus on when he disappears?"

I was silent. Walker was on target. The Feds would suspect me, and they would descend upon me like a pack of rabid wolves—the imagery was ironically amusing—when Darke stopped checking in. And since there was no way of knowing how often Darke had been expected to report to his superiors, the Feds could be preparing to come after me right now. No wonder Walker said I had gotten stupid. Maybe he was right.

"Okay," I finally answered. That reassuring whiskey gauze had disappeared. "When do you want to do it?"

He shot me a disappointed look. I sighed. "Yeah, that's what I figured. See you the night after tomorrow."

Ivan smiled and shook his head. The pentangle-shaped scar on his neck jiggled softly with the movement. "No, we're not going to wait that long. We'll snatch him tomorrow night."

"But the moon won't be full until the night after." Tom Waits growled on the Wurlitzer juke, adding to the sense of hopelessness and desolation I was feeling. I had to go up against Ton Ton Philippe again. What were the odds I could survive the confrontation a second time?

"Exactly," Walker said.

"I'm not following you. Why would we go after Ton Ton before a full moon?"

Walker shook his head sadly. "Come on, mate, think about it. Philippe is going to torture Darke until the Fed spills his guts about why he's here in The City. No matter how tough he is, Darke will talk eventually. Once the fat Haitian fuck finds out Darke is here because of you, he'll hold onto him and try to figure out how to use that information to his advantage."

I spread my hands, frustrated. "I understand all that. I just don't know why we would go into the Pink Pussy before I've changed, rather than one night later, when at least we'll stand a fighting chance."

"That's where you're wrong," Walker said. "Philippe knows you'll be trying to spring Darke, you have no choice. He'll be expecting you to do it in two nights, when the moon is full. By then he'll be surrounded by every zombie and human fighter in his crew. You won't stand a chance. It'll be a bloodbath.

"But he'll never expect an attack tomorrow night," my former partner continued. "All we need is a diversion, and we can go into Philippe's stronghold, pluck the Fed right out from under the fat bastard's nose, and be gone before he realizes what's happening."

I thought about it. Ivan was right. It made sense. Except… "How are we going to manage a diversion?"

Walker grinned like the cat that ate not just a canary but a whole flock of them. "We don't have to. Otto Rhino is going to take care of that for us."

Count Otto Rhino was Ton Ton Philippe's biggest underworld rival, constantly fighting the Haitian for control of The City. "Why would Rhino do that?"

"Because I let slip in front of the department's most reliable Rhino mole that Philippe's stronghold is going to be ripe for the plucking tonight, that he's stored three hundred keys of heroin in the Pink Pussy nightclub and that virtually every one of his men will be down on the waterfront bringing in more. I let it slip that tonight's the only night Ton Ton's place will be unguarded."

I felt my pulse begin to race and my mood brighten just a bit. It could work. "Rhino's guys will be totally unprepared."

"That's right."

"Let's do it."

The air hanging over The City was hot and stagnant; it smelled like dirty socks and unwashed bodies, like stolen innocence and abandoned dreams. It always did. The occasional breeze bold enough to fight its way through The City's smog and grime felt more like an assault than any kind of refreshment.

Walker and I talked little, perched atop the Pink Pussy, the one-time gothic church converted into a club and also home base for Ton Ton Philippe's ever-expanding criminal empire. Afer finalizing our plan at Duffy's, we had both hurried home to catch a few hours of needed rest before meeting down the street from Philippe's club just before daybreak. Walker set a ladder against the rear of the building, away from prying eyes, not that there were any at that time of day, then we scaled the walls and made ourselves as comfortable as possible.

A few minutes later, one of Walker's cop cronies, a man I didn't know, came by and removed the ladder, placing it quietly in the back of an unmarked van and disappearing. And we were in position.

The day dragged and we alternately dozed and kept watch, although it was clear nothing would happen until late at night. I tried to remain sharp by reviewing what I knew of the Pink Pussy's interior. The altar of the cathedral had been walled off and converted into Ton Ton Philippe's office, an abomination if you were the church-going sort, but the perfect arrangement if you wanted to drop in unannounced.

Constructed directly above the altar was what at one time had been the choir loft, where a massive pipe organ had issued heavenly strains of music to consecrated ears. A series of skylight windows had been built into the ceiling to allow as much natural light into the space as possible. The skylights had long since been bricked over, but would offer little resistance to the twelve-pound mauls Walker and I had lugged onto the roof. Or so we hoped.

Finally night fell and shortly thereafter, crowds began to file into Ton Ton Philippe's club. I had begun to feel lethargic as the hours passed, but now adrenaline started to kick in. Ivan and I watched and especially listened as revelers came and went. We didn't know when to expect the assault by the Frog Boys—Otto Rhino's troops—but understood we would have precious little time to take advantage of the distraction when it occurred.

Finally it did.

The screams were the first indication that the Frog Boys had entered the building. The sound was high-pitched and frantic, girlish, even from the men, and seconds later, the stutter of automatic gunfire ripped through the night. Ivan and I got to work. Nobody spoke. Nobody had to.

We grabbed our mauls and attacked the bricks, taking great, full swings, smashing the twelve-pound iron heads onto the bricks, and within seconds the ancient mortar begin to give way. Soon bricks were dropping into the choir pit, falling onto the floor with echoing thuds we hoped would be swallowed up by the panicked sounds of confusion and fear and destruction.

I knew Walker hoped the automatic gunfire was only meant to frighten the partiers, to force a stampede out the club's front entrance so that the attackers could make their assault on Philippe's fortified office. My friend and former partner was risking his career for me, a sacrifice I could never hope to repay.

I wiped sweat from my eyes and glanced at Walker, who barked, "Get back to work," almost as if he could read my mind. He was right, of course—we had only minutes to make this play work and the time for reflection would be when we were finished. If we survived.

A few more swings and my arms burned with the effort, but more importantly, Ivan and I had opened a gaping hole roughly three feet by three feet in the old church's roof directly over the location where the pipe organ had once exhorted the righteous and pure with heavenly music, but which now sat silent and dusty, lost to a world God had seemingly abandoned.

Ivan had secured a long rope on a winch to one of the old church's soaring spires hours ago, and now I tossed the coiled loop through the hole and onto the floor of the choir pit, shimmying down as the tone of the screams coming from below began to change. Clearly, Rhino's men had discovered that Philippe's place wasn't mostly unguarded like they had been led to believe, and the battle wasn't going well. Screams of pain began mingling with those of fear, and I wondered how long the Frog Boys could hold out before they were all killed or abandoned the assault and took off in an all-out retreat.

Ivan dropped a five-foot iron pry bar through the hole, and it clattered on the floor of the choir loft like thunder. I hoped the noise would get lost in the general chaos and confusion echoing through the Pink Pussy. I pried up a wide pine floorboard and it shrieked in protest, the sound eerily similar to the screams coming from one floor below. I tossed the board aside and pried up another, repeating the process a third time until I had opened up a slash wide enough to lower myself through. Then I kicked out a panel of the false ceiling to Ton Ton's office, hoping—I had stopped praying years ago—that the Haitian voodoo master would want to keep Agent Darke near, where he could work on the man whenever the inspiration struck.

And I was right. The ceiling panel smashed into pieces on the floor of Ton Ton's office as I stared into the devastation below. Zombies were locked in pitched combat with Rhino's men, all of whom were enormous and who seemed to be handling themselves more skillfully than I would have predicted.

But even better than that was one unexpected lucky break: The spot I had chosen—entirely at random—to break through the ceiling of Ton Ton's office was located directly above a makeshift prison cell constructed, presumably, to hold me, but which at the moment held the prone body of Agent Darke, the kidnapped Fed.

He lay on the floor, wrists and ankles tied with sturdy twine, reacting sluggishly to the mayhem around him, clearly drugged but just as clearly alive. A hazy smoke filled the interior of Philippe's office and the voodoo priest himself was nowhere to be seen. If his past history was any indication, Philippe had vanished at the first sign of hostilities.

I tossed the rope through the hole and shimmied down, dropping with a thud next to Darke, whose dull eyes widened with recognition at the sight of me. "You," he slurred. I ignored him. Incredibly, no one on either side of the fight taking place outside Darke's prison cell seemed to have noticed my arrival, and I wanted to milk that advantage for every second I could.

I picked Darke up at the waist and tossed his hogtied body over my shoulder, wishing I could take advantage of the super-human strength I would possess in less than twenty-four hours. The man was a heavy dead weight. I staggered to the rope and wrapped one hand and one foot around it and screamed to Walker, waiting two stories above, "Go!"

And that got the attention of one of Ton Ton's zombies. His back had been to the bars as he fought hand to hand with one of the Frog Boys, a misshapen giant with arms that appeared to be as long as my legs. The zombie turned at the sound of my scream and dropped the knife he had been holding, picking a handgun up off the floor and sighting down the barrel at Darke and me.

We weren't going to make it. Walker had flipped the power switch on the winch the moment I yelled up to him, but the damned thing was pulling us too slowly. We had barely left the ground. We hung helplessly a foot off the floor, moving upward with agonizing slowness. The zombie smiled—a hideous sight if you've never experienced it—and I closed my eyes and waited to be blown off the rope.

And nothing happened.

I opened my eyes a second later, just in time to see the zombie's head toppling off his shoulders and onto the floor, sliced cleanly from his body by the giant's massive sword. He stared at me uncomprehendingly as another of Ton Ton's boys rushed to the cell bars, screaming something unintelligible. The punk reached through the bars at us, his grasping fingers too short by inches. He either didn't have a gun or didn't think to use it.

A moment later he didn't have a head, either, as I watched the giant slice it off, making a matching set of zombie heads on the floor of Ton Ton Philippe's office. Then the winch pulled us through the ceiling and upward to freedom.

The overaged barflies were back at Duffy's, again trying to monopolize the Wurlitzer, but this time Duffy was having none of it. He was engaged in an animated conversation with them—it occurred to me how much they resembled Ton Ton's zombies and I shuddered—and although I couldn't hear what was being said, I could pretty well guess. A moment later the pair stomped out in a huff and Duffy returned behind the bar with a smug smile on his face.

Walker and I were sharing a celebratory drink despite the hour—it was barely noon—and our exhaustion. We had cut Agent Darke out of his bindings and thrown him into the front seat of his strange black car where we had found it parked at the curb a short distance from the Pink Pussy. He was going to have one hell of a headache but appeared basically unharmed.

"What do you suppose happens now?" I said.

"You mean with Darke?" my friend asked, and I nodded. "I guess he drives on back wherever he came from and lets his superiors know there's a lot more going on in The City than any-one realized."

"I mean regarding me, specifically."

Walker shrugged. "You said he recognized you, so he knows you saved his life. That's gotta count for something. You'll prob-ably just have to take it day by day, see what happens next."

"That's what I always do."

"It's all anyone can do," Walker said, and looked me over closely. "You look like hell."

"It's been a busy couple of days."

"It's more than that," Walker said, and he was right. I could feel the itch of the coming Change under my skin, the incessant, ancient, irresistible urge that would soon overtake my body, and would do so every lunar cycle for the rest of my life. I thought about Ton Ton's zombie sighting down the barrel of his gun at me and how close I had come to being blown away.

And I wondered whether I was lucky or cursed that it hadn't happened.

Allan Leverone is the author of the thrillers *Final Vector*, *The Lonely Mile*, and *Pasagankee*, as well as the horror novel-las *Darkness Falls* and *Heartless*. He is a four-time Derringer Award finalist as well as a 2011 Puschcart Prize nominee whose short fiction has been featured in *Needle: A Magazine of Noir*, *Shotgun Honey*, *Shroud Magazine*, *Dark Valentine*, *Morpheus Tales*, and many others. Connect with Allan on Facebook, Twitter (@AllanLeverone), or at www.allanleverone.com.

IT'S A CURSE

K.A. Laity

I COULD FEEL MY EYEBALLS roll in their sockets before I opened my lids: never a good sign. I steeled myself for the brutal fact of daylight, but the dawn was as grey as if it hadn't yet decided to get dressed. I reached for the crumpled pack of gaspers lying next to the bed. The object my groping fingers found puzzled me.

I opened one eye warily. It was a handkerchief, floral and trimmed in lace. The table beneath it was a similarly lacy object, a cascade of flounces that made it look like a lost wedding cake. My dull brain raised and then dismissed the idea of lunatic-by-night decorators. My lids closed again as I stifled a groan.

"Roman? You awake?"

I tried not to stiffen at her words, but it was no use. I grunted.

"You want some coffee?" Her voice made it a question, but I could feel her shifting off the bed to go make some. The springs squealed slightly as she dismounted. Her soft footsteps headed away from the bedroom.

I willed myself to return to the lethean embrace of Morpheus, but he decided to respond with a sledgehammer between my eyebrows. A fist pressed to my forehead did little to assuage the assault. A second front opened in my mouth: suffocation by sponge. I pried one lid open and spotted a squat glass resting on the lacy table with a mouthful of bourbon left in it.

Gingerly I raised myself on one elbow and made a shaky grab for the tumbler as sirens screeched inside my skull. It wasn't much, but that mouthful of bourbon fought back the cottony feeling in my throat even as my belly winced. I lurched out of the bed and found myself clad only in a vest and pants. Staggering to the bathroom sink, I saw a wreck of a man staring at me from the mirror with red eyes and a sour expression.

Cold water braced me somewhat, though a spell of dizziness overtook me. I calculated the time left before the full moon and decided it must have only been rotgut that laid me low. I opened the medicine cabinet and found a small bottle of aspirin and shook a few into my hand. The refilled glass offered a hint of bourbon as I washed them down.

I found the rest of my clothes neatly folded on a chair by the bed, which suggested I hadn't put them there. This morning just got better and better. The clank of my belt as I poked myself into my trousers echoed in my ears like a church bell and I sat heavily on the bed, willing the pounding to stop.

I had got to buttoning my shirt when she came back, two steaming mugs of coffee on a tray. "I didn't know how you take it," she said, a smile like a kicked dog's cringe across her face. A small creamer shaped like a cow sat next to a sugar bowl that looked like a strawberry.

"Thanks," I finally muttered. Sucking down the black java jolted my corpse back to life sufficiently to regard my Samaritan. I knew her. Mabel: cornfed, cornflower-blue eyes, pink cheeks far too healthy for a low-life dive like Duffy's, but I'd seen her there before, drifting on the fringes. Some religious nut, no doubt, I guessed, come from the heartland to save the big-city sinners. It formed the bones of a very old story, one that always ended badly.

"I'm late." I upended the cup, and its black tar burned the rest of the cotton away. At least her coffee wasn't church-going. I threw on my jacket and shrugged a goodbye.

"See you 'round," she said, her voice brimming with hope and her eyes too bright with something even more dangerous.

"Sure, sure." My temples pounded a symphony that had me nodding as if in assent. I grabbed my hat and edged toward the egress.

"Thanks for saving my life."

I hurried out the door without answering and staggered down the steps to the filthy streets.

"Coffee? Or are you ready to start oiling your neck again?" Duffy flipped the battered *National Geographic* over on the counter so that the unnaturally green frog smiled upside down from the cover as I sat on a stool.

"Coffee." I wished I had thrown a few more aspirins down my gullet but another cup ought to sort that out. Duffy's java had about five times the strength of a normal brew. He claimed the beans had come from his cousin the alchemist. On days like this, I almost believed him.

He slid a mug across the counter and grinned a little too widely in its wake. "So, we gonna hear some wedding bells soon?"

A growl rumbled in my throat. The full moon was still days off, but the wolf already ran under my skin. He never really left anymore.

"Come on, Roman. You were awfully friendly with her last night."

This time I did snarl. "I don't remember a thing."

Duffy grinned. "You missed a good show. Those metal jockeys never had a chance."

I let the hot black blast fill my throat and ignored him. The wasps in my head were beginning to drown at last, and a little silence would have aided their demise. Unfortunately Duffy blathered on, a pointless tale of drunken boasts, a damsel in distress, and damage to the furniture that he blamed on me.

"Mr. Dalton, I presume?"

I swiveled my neck to the right, a mistake, as the wasps took flight once more. "Who wants to know?"

He was tall and trim, clad in a Saville Row suit worn with such utter carelessness that he had to have been born to it. Sandy brown hair topped a face with the bluest eyes I'd ever seen and an amused look that its wearer probably never lost. He took a drag on a Gauloise and favoured me with a broad smile that managed not to suggest any sort of friendliness. "Edward Jameson."

"You're a long way from home, Mr. Jameson. Why didn't you send your butler instead?"

One eyebrow raised just enough to deepen the picture of amusement. "It's a rather delicate matter. My butler and I have a little understanding; he pretends not to know all my intimate secrets and I pretend to believe him. May I sit down?"

"Suit yourself." I held the mug out and Duffy refueled me. I wasn't eager for a new job but my bank balance would be happy to remind me that my dance card needed filling.

"I would like you to find my sister," Jameson said in a voice low enough to suggest that this was not information on general offer.

But it was the wrong thing to say. Duffy snorted, and I shot him a look that had a few wasps clinging to it and he shut up. "If you want me to find some floozy, you just say so. I'm not going to think any less of you."

Jameson frowned. "I want you to find my sister, Beryl Jameson, and persuade her to return home." He reached into the breast pocket of that slate-grey suit and pulled out a photo. There was no doubt about their relation. The crisp black-and-white image offered the same high cheekbones and big eyes that looked a lot more fetching on her features. Her lips had the same arrogant, amused smile, too. On that face, however, it looked like sauce you'd want to taste. "I'm afraid we find ourselves up against a sort of deadline as well."

"Already booked the holidays in Tuscany?" Duffy said over the Nat Geo, chortling at his own wit.

"I can see how you worked your way up to the apex of your field," Jameson murmured, a cold smile on his face, but his eyes on me. "There's a wedding."

"Does she know that?"

"Indeed." A flicker of irritation mixed with genuine pain strobed across his face. "She has showed a remarkable lack of interest in the proceedings."

"Maybe she can just send a gift. I hear pizza stones are popular."

Jameson exhaled a cloud of smoke. "It's her wedding."

It had to be my imagination, but I could have sworn the smile in her picture got a little more devilish. "Could be she's changed her mind."

"I don't think so."

"Some other guy? Or girl?" I shrugged.

"No."

I studied the lines of his face. "You seem awfully certain."

"I know my sister." Jameson stubbed out his cigarette in the tray, which looked like a can-can dancer. "If Beryl had decided to call off the wedding, she would have had no qualms about saying so. There's something else going on."

"She won't return your calls?"

"Beryl's not answering calls. She's not in her flat. That's why I want you to find her." The irritation bled through the careful cool mask of his face. Funny how a few minutes talking with me seemed to always bring that out in people.

"Do you have any idea where she might be? Or should I just start buttonholing saps on the street?"

"I understand you know the sort of places that people go when they don't want to be found. That is why I was told to contact you." The icy look on his face would have filled a martini shaker and left plenty over for a highball.

"Does she have any known vices? It helps to have someplace to start. Gambling? Dope? Drink? Nude pachinko?"

Jameson's big blue eyes had dark lashes that looked a lot better on his sister, but they kept the threat in his gaze from getting too warm. "She's not above a little flutter now and again. The relaxed ambience of a casino might suit her."

"It gives me a place to start," I agreed with a rusty smile.

"I suppose this will start you off on your travels," Jameson said as he handed me a cheque with a pleasing number of digits and an embossed card. "Phone me when you find her."

"Pedophile," Duffy muttered as Jameson walked out the door, carefully avoiding contact with anything in the bar.

"You're just not used to posh people," I said, holding my cup out for a last refill. "You have a prejudice, Duffy."

He shook his head and tapped a finger on the green frog. "Something's not right about him. You best take care."

"His cabbage looks right enough." I squinted at the cheque in the dim light. "I've got no complaints with a man who pays well."

"All the same—"

"You wouldn't invite him home for a meal with the family?"

"Yeah."

"Noted." I swallowed the last of the java and slipped off my chair. "Time to earn that paycheck." I almost felt human again. Pity I wasn't.

"No, never seen her." The hunchback left a greasy print on the edge of the photograph when I tugged it from his grip. "I'd remember that."

I tried to ignore the way he licked his lips. His tongue oozed out like a diseased slug, leaving a glistening trail behind it. "You know any new underground games afoot? Something good if you wanted to hide your predilections?"

"You're not talking about Ton-Ton's joint, eh?" His sneer grew. "I hear you're none too welcome there." The hunchback wiped his palm on his waistcoat with lascivious pleasure. "Not welcome at all."

"I got bad manners, what can I say? You got any suggestions?"

He chuckled. It sounded as if he were chewing on a small furry animal desperately trying to escape its fate. The pong that wafted up from his teeth made the possibility seem less remote. "I dunno. People say things, but you know, I don't always listen that close."

Aw, poor fella. He is not appreciated. I greased his palm a little further, not that it needed much. "Maybe that'll jog your memory a bit. I have the feeling something's just popped into your recollection."

"Well," he admitted, "I did hear rumours of the pikey starting up a new floater in the Marquis, that old cha-cha palace."

Pikey? "You mean Marinova? I didn't know she was back." I couldn't decide if that was good news or not. "Fast work if she's got the Marquis renovated."

He shrugged. "Like I said, it's something I heard. Maybe your fancy filly turned up for the grand opening."

"Thanks. You've been helpful."

The hunchback grinned and rubbed his hand on his waistcoat again. "I'm always glad to pocket a little extra dosh." He hopped up from his stool to open the door for a smart-suited businessman who saved a disapproving look for me, which seemed unfair, given the present company. "I got a lot of time on my hands."

I nodded and headed out into the street. The past three days had been a bust with a lot of pavement pounding and very little luck. The moon was getting fatter but my leads had stayed thin. I wasn't sure how Marinova would greet me, but it seemed the most promising trail so far. In no time I stood before the old hotel. The corpse looked lively. The façade showed its age, but a considerable crew patrolled its entrance.

I buttonholed a mug I knew slightly. "O'Connell, is Marinova in?"

The Irishman looked at me with some doubt. "You sure she wants to see you? I seem to recall a little contretemps between you and her cousin, or was it her brother—?"

"Water under the bridge," I assured him. What's a few dead bodies between friends, after all? "She in?"

O'Connell shrugged. "In the casino room, I expect. But you want to be careful there, Roman. The pikey's got a long memory and she's not keen on interference."

"Who's interfering? I'm just looking up an old friend. And I don't think she much appreciates being referred to as a pikey. She comes from a long and illustrious line of travelers."

O'Connell's face fell. "You know I was only saying it in fun—"

I nodded. "Sure, sure. I'll keep it to myself, nothing to worry about."

Leaving the Irishman sweating, I waltzed through the reception area, dodging workmen carrying a new roll of carpet. It looked like Marinova had intentions of doing the place up right; she must want to lure the uptown crowd down here as well as the suburbanites across the river. Someone had a whole lot of folding money. The plan made me idly curious, but not enough to lose track of my aim here.

I headed up the rich red-carpeted steps to the ballroom and saw a splendour that dazzled. It glowed like a little bit of Monte Carlo in the midst of this seedy neighbourhood, one that had seen better years but not since my Great-Aunt Fanny's day.

I found Marinova near the baccarat tables. Her black hair fell in its usual tumble, but she wore a cocktail dress that made the most of her ripe curves. I decided on the amnesia approach. "Well, Marinova! Of all the gin joints in all the towns in all the world—"

Her expression remained unreadable as she turned to regard me. "Roman Dalton, how you have changed."

I shrugged. "A little more mileage on the meter, that's all."

She smiled and walked right up to me and took my hand in hers, then stared intently at my palm. "Changed indeed."

I tried to pull my fingers from her grip without success. "I'm looking for someone, maybe you've seen her?"

Marinova dropped my hand then and gave me a strange smile. "And why should I help you, Roman Dalton?"

"You're such a good-hearted woman, how can you resist?"

She laughed. It was a warm sound, one that gave me unreasonable hope. Her words offered less encouragement. "I think rather you owe me a little something extra."

"Maybe I can cut you in on this deal if you help me out." I had no idea how that might work, but I always found it easier to promise good intentions than to deliver them. "There's plenty of money at stake, and it looks like you're burning through an awful lot of it here."

A waitress appeared with a tray and two glasses of pale green-ish liquid. I wondered how she had been summoned. Marinova took the glasses and handed one to me. "*Na zdrowie.*"

"Better days." I tipped the glass back and the zubrowka warmed my throat. The thought crossed my mind that it might not be my health we were drinking to, but I knew it would be fatal to hesitate with her.

"My better days are here," the dark beauty said. "I think yours may be behind you."

I tried to hide my irritation. "What's that? A gypsy curse? I got plenty of better days ahead."

"How many until the moon is full?" Her eyes were black as midnight, and I found their gaze too much to endure.

"Why should I care? I'm no stargazer. Listen, there's this bird I gotta find, might be here. A real thoroughbred type, swanky pedigree, family the kind who hunts little critters on bigger ones."

"My target clientele," Marinova said with a laugh. "I'm keeping the miscreants like you out of this place. Every level requires more money, fewer allowed in. People yearn for exclusivity. I promise it."

"I'll get my tux out of mothballs," I muttered. I dug in my pocket for the picture now sporting the hunchback's fingerprint. "You ever see this beauty? Her brother's looking to squire her home again. The family misses her terribly."

Marinova did not look at the picture. "If she doesn't want to go home, why should she?"

I lifted my palms up in innocence. "I'm not going to force her. I get paid to find her. If she don't want to come home, I tell her family so. They just want to know. No funny business, no commotion."

She looked at me with something that felt an awful lot like pity. "Try the penthouse lounge."

"You're a queen among women." I pocketed the picture and turned to go.

"And you're a beast among men, Roman Dalton." Marinova spoke softly but the words hit like a blow anyway. I hunched my shoulders and walked on, the zubrowka churning my guts yet. When I reached the lifts, I punched the button with a little more energy than it called for to summon one. The wolf arched in my spine. His time drew closer. I hit the button again. I needed to finish up this job.

When the doors opened at the top of the shaft, opulence greeted me. If the room below seemed well-appointed, the lounge offered a crowning achievement. Every bit of it gleamed with well-polished wood and metal. The colours of the walls and furniture came from a muted palette that suggested soft voices and murmured conversation: the kind of dosh that never had to raise its voice to be heard. I ignored the waiter who looked at me as if I had been rolled there by some sort of dung beetle. There was a platinum head at the end of the long oak bar with just the right arrogant tilt to it to be Beryl Jameson.

I made my way across the silk carpet to the curve of the bar where she sat on a tall silver chair. Jameson wore a slinky dress that hugged her shape like a jealous husband, but she would have looked just as good in a gunny sack. Doubtless she'd look best in nothing but a hair ribbon. I would have admired the view a little longer but I was beginning to feel conspicuous as I passed the swells. "Beryl Jameson?"

Her head turned toward me, a smirk on her lips and an ebony cigarette holder in her hand. I was right; the big blue eyes looked better on her than on her brother, the long dark lashes shading the startling colour as if it were too much for mere mortals. But it was her perfume that got me by the throat and raised all the hairs on the back of my neck. The wolf's heart thudded in my chest with an unfamiliar ache. It took all my power not to growl and leap on her right then. Sweat sprang out on my forehead and my collar became too tight.

"No one but my family calls me Beryl," she said, her voice a contralto copy of her brother's, with the same languorous insouciance. Her gaze traveled up and down me. No doubt she'd want to wash her eyes afterward. "They want me dragged back there, don't they?"

I affected innocence again. "No one suggested dragging you. I'm just here to request that you consider the possibility. Nothing more."

Beryl laughed. Her friends regarded me with expressions normally reserved for pervs in the kiddie park. "What's going to persuade me?"

"Maybe we could talk private like for a minute?"

"Don't go, Lil." The young Beau Brummell at her side laid a manicured hand on her arm. A glance from her made him withdraw the hand at once.

"I'll be all right over here," she said, nodding her head toward a booth in the corner. "A couple of pink gins for my consultant and me, Josef." Jameson slipped off her chair and walked over to the table. I followed the sway of her hips like a mesmerist's pigeon. It was all I could do not to let my tongue hang out like some Tex Avery cartoon. I wasn't sure why I was so hot and bothered. Must have been the perfume. Or maybe it was the lack of action for many a moon.

I let her sit first, then slid down on the opposite side. "I appreciate your giving me a chance to talk."

She shrugged. "They want me to come back. I'm not going back."

I nodded to show I was not an unreasonable guy. "Your brother said something about a wedding." I looked down at the rock on her hand. It could have cooled a high ball with ease.

Jameson looked up as the bartender brought the drinks on a silver tray. "Thank you, Josef." She slid one across the table to me. "*Slainté.*"

As she tipped her head back to drink, all I could think about was how much I wanted to fasten my teeth around her neck and make her whimper. I shook myself and downed the better part of my drink. It wasn't half bad, but I had a feeling it might not settle well on top of the Polish vodka. "It would be a shame to disappoint all those guests."

Her brow furrowed. "What's your name?"

"Dalton. Roman Dalton."

"What's your story, Dalton?"

"One as old as the world. Just an honest man in the world he never made."

She barked a quick laugh. "Honest!" The puzzled look returned. "You're a detective."

I nodded. "I'd say I preferred dick, but I get called that a little too much to enjoy it, Miss Jameson."

"Lil." Jameson smiled, then looked thoughtful. "There's something odd about you."

"I missed the Paris fashions this year, so I'm out of season. Imagine my embarrassment."

"You're not what you seem."

"Neither are you." I couldn't say why my heart was racing again. I downed the last of the gin. It probably didn't help.

"I'm not going back. They wouldn't understand."

"Money: They can pay. Drugs: They can sort it out. You got a lover? They can probably manage that as well. Nothing much that can't be dealt with. That's what money's for." I kept the bitterness out of my voice almost completely.

"It's not like that," she said, turning her head away. "You don't know how it is. You wouldn't understand."

"Try me. I've seen some pretty strange stuff in my time. Things you wouldn't believe."

"Why do you smell like that?"

I blinked. "You don't like a smoker?"

Jameson leaned over the table and sniffed at me. "That's not smoke."

"I don't know what you mean, I—"

"Let's go to my suite. We can't talk here."

I nodded, flummoxed. Without a word she stood up and darted toward the exit. I trotted behind her as she slammed her hand onto the call button. On the ride down, her fingers drummed rapidly on her crossed arms, but she stayed on the far side of the car and did not speak. We got off on the ninth floor and she let us into the first room down the corridor.

I'd barely stepped inside the door when she slammed it behind me, threw her clutch on the low table and spun around. "What are you?" she hissed. I didn't get a chance to answer because Lil launched herself at me and bit my neck. We went down together, growls erupting from our throats.

I rolled her over so I was on top once again. I grabbed the collar of her dress to pull it off her shoulder and bite her breast. Lil howled and fought back, hands scrabbling at my shirt as buttons flew across the carpet. Her nails raked my chest and I sucked the air in surprise. I shoved her dress up in search of that intoxicating scent and buried my face between her thighs.

Her hands ripped at my clothes and hair as she struggled against me. Rolling across the floor we fought, her teeth on my chest as I tried to pin her down. When I finally managed to wiggle out of my trousers, she was ready for me and pulled me on top of her, sinking her teeth into my shoulder as I sank into her. We howled together, a wild and desperate threnody, as the beasts in us merged.

I awoke about three, for once without the piercing spike of a hangover in my brain. I savoured the feeling with relief for a moment, then I moved and became aware of the aches that tortured my flesh. I could see the purple marks of bruises on my shoulders where Lil's teeth had found a hold. My shins were barked, and long-unused muscles screamed their complaints as I rolled out of bed to take a piss. The wee man had some complaints of his own, feeling raw and red as I winced over the bowl. How many times had it been?

Limping back to the bed, I found Lil deep asleep yet. My rough digits had left deep bruises on her arms and thighs. They looked black in the moonlight, My teeth had marked her throat. Nonetheless she looked peaceful enough in her slumber and snuggled against me as I slipped back under the covers. I decided not to think about anything at all and willed myself back to sleep with one arm crooked around her waist. It was the sweetest oblivion I had tasted in some time—maybe ever.

The sun decided to hide its head that day, which was just as well when we surfaced about noon. I woke to the drumming of the rain outside and a steady gaze from those remarkably blue eyes. "You're not so much in the morning light."

"You, on the other hand, are a peach." I touched the purple on her throat with a finger. "A bruised peach, but a peach nonetheless."

"I finally meet another wolf, and he's a middle-aged ex-cop with a bad attitude." Lil shook her head.

"How'd you know I was an ex-cop?"

She laughed. "Aren't all you shamuses ex-cops?"

"Shamus? Listen to the society bird sling the lingo." She tweaked my nipple and I yelped. "So how'd it happen?"

Sighing, she lay back on the pillows. "Would you believe up on the moors? The ancestral home. It's like something out of a

Brontë tale. I was just hacking along, trying to think about where everything went wrong. It came out of nowhere. Or Scotland. I hear that's the home of the original Big Bad Wolf." She laughed: a flat, mirthless sound. "Pulled me off my horse. Tore through my clothes. I thought I was dead. Then I woke up." Lil laid an arm across her eyes. "You?"

"Bikers in a bar fight."

She laughed but there wasn't much humour in it. "Get me some gin and a ciggie, will you?" I rolled out of bed and padded over to the minibar. I poured a whisky for myself as well and lit two cigarettes. Lil sat up. I handed her the tumbler of gin and put the coffin nail to her lips. She inhaled deeply. "Bloody buggery bollocks, innit?"

"Yep." I blew out a cloud of smoke and sipped the whisky.

"Let's paint the town red tonight, shamus. One last time."

I looked at her pale face and those big blue eyes. "Whatever you say, partner."

"Hey, that Mabel was looking for you," Duffy said as he emptied the can-can girl ashtray under the big silver star, which seemed to have picked up some new cobwebs this week. "You want I should call her over to take care of you?" He chortled, ignoring my growl. "I hope the other guy looks worse."

"That Jameson been by at all?"

Duffy rummaged under the bar. "He called, ah, let's see. Yesterday." He consulted the crumpled note. "Wanting to know if you'd made any progress."

I settled myself down on a stool, wincing. "Yeah. I made progress. Gimme some whisky to celebrate." I lit another cigarette and reached for the glass. No matter I'd already oiled my neck enough to be feeling no pain. I was counting down the hours until sunset, a time I'd come to dread. But not tonight. Tonight would be gangbusters.

"Jesus, Roman. You look weird. And done in." Duffy tutted as he refilled the glass.

"You just never seen me happy before." I could feel my grin getting a little sloppy but I was past caring. I took a long drag on my cigarette and enjoyed being alive for a moment. I should have known it couldn't last.

"Roman?" Her voice grated like a pair of heels dragged over pavement. "You busy?"

"I'm always busy," I growled. Last thing I needed. No whinging zombies, no bargain vampires, and certainly no well-meaning do-gooders.

"I just thought we might talk for a minute." The worst part had to be her smile in that too-soft face. It made me want to push it right through the other side of her head. I hunched my shoulders. The wolf had little patience today.

"Listen, Mabel. I know you're glad to be alive and all, but that don't mean there's something between us."

"You seemed to want some comfort the other night," she said, laying her soft white hand on my rumpled sleeve. "I can help fight the evil within you. You can win."

I shrugged off her touch. "It's a curse. It's not a moral failing, I'm not a lost soul. The world is fucked-up, and there's no silver lining that doesn't come with a bullet. Go back to Wisconsin."

"Michigan," Mabel whispered.

"Whatever." I swallowed the last of the whisky and slid the glass back to Duffy for a refill. "You stick around here and you're going to get hurt." I turned my back on her in a way that I hoped made it clear I had no intention of turning around again. I didn't need to see that big lower lip tremble or see tears in those eyes. Their blue could not match Lil's crystalline beauty. I wanted to pull the night around me like a cowl. Duffy regarded me without a word as he poured out more of that low-rent elixir.

"You got no heart, Roman."

I picked up the glass and drained it. "You gotta be cruel to be kind. Nothing less than the truth. This town will chew her bones. Besides, I got a date."

"Not mixing work with pleasure again?" Duffy arched an eyebrow at me. "Remember how it went last time."

"It's not like that. This is different, a whole other galaxy altogether." I held out the glass again.

After a long look, Duffy poured a little more. "You might want to go easy on the sauce—especially tonight, Roman. If the last few months are anything to go by, heads are gonna roll."

I waved away his concerns. "I'm staying out of trouble tonight. No strife, no hoodlums. Just a big night out with a woman who understands the beast in me." I saluted Duffy and headed out the door into the late afternoon sun. The wolf in me stretched his limbs and prepared for release.

She met me at my place. I figured it was safer. We'd be off the streets. Lil looked around the flat and gave me an amused grin. "Spartan."

"Hey, I've gone all out on the hospitality front," I complained. "Clean glasses, clean sheets." I handed her a tumbler of the good stuff from a newly popped bottle of gin. "Nothing but the best."

She took the glass. The ice clinked against the sides. "You ought to get some bitters."

"I'll add it to my shopping list," I said, looking at her over the rim of my glass, trying to keep the wolf in check a few minutes longer. The suspense rested like a ball of fire in my gut, one the whisky couldn't still.

"It comes over like an itch at first, doesn't it?" Lil's eyes seemed bigger in the dusk, wet with something that wasn't tears. "From the inside." She downed the gin with a grimace, then with no further preamble shrugged off her dress to stand naked before me, her breasts like twin moons filling my brain. I dropped my glass and pounced. We rolled across the floor trading bites and yips, tails entwining and raw howls of lust gurgling from our throats. For once, the wolf was happy.

I should have known it wouldn't be enough.

We coupled and rested and did it all again. And then she looked at me with those yellow eyes and laughed, and we sank a few more drinks and hit the streets. After a time I can't remember much. The night was long, the drinks and the blood flowed freely, we ate well. You wouldn't miss most of the lowlifes we mowed down in our drunken spree. Honestly, we were doing the city a favour. We cleaned up more recalcitrants in a night than the men in blue had in the last six months.

But yeah, I felt bad about Mabel. Some days, everything hurts. The tabloids printed those pictures of her head sitting on the flower box in my neighbour's window, that look of surprise on her face. I know there will be nights when I wake up defending myself to that face.

Duffy tried to be sympathetic. "You did warn her. I suppose she ought to have listened." He folded over the *National Geographic* with the Peruvian snails on the cover, nudging the overfilled ashtray aside. "It don't get no easier, does it?"

I nodded and shoved my glass over for a refill. My head was full of hornets again. I ached in every joint and limb. The bruises on my neck and face would heal. The whisky helped. Not enough, of course, but it did its part to numb the dull ache of it all. I could have done without the blaring box, where some breathless society sycophant panted after the thoroughbred couple as they announced their happy news before ranks of dignitaries and relatives. The scarf around her neck hid a lot, but her smile was lupine. I had a feeling the wedding night would be memorable, at least for her.

"You want I should turn that off?" Duffy asked solicitously, which somehow made it even worse.

"Nah, it happens. Right?"

"It's a curse," Duffy said, topping up my glass again.

"That it is, that it is."

———

K.A. Laity writes just about any damn thing she pleases and that's how she got where she is today: living the high life in Galway on the Fulbright Foundation's dime. See her website at www.kalaity. com for a full list of publications, including novels, short stories, plays, humour, academic essays, and even the odd poem. Find her on Facebook and Twitter, or just buy her a drink at the pub around the corner.

INSATIABLE

B.R. Stateham

I felt it.

Like a thousand needles suddenly thrust into your body.

Like electricity, millions of volts, searing across every nerve ending in a white heat of raw energy. Like an insatiable hunger overpowering you—blinding you—overwhelming you in an urgent, mindless, desire to feed.

That time of the month. The change. When the moon becomes full and the wolves of the forest lift their haunting voices up to pay homage to the goddess of the night. The moon would be full in two nights. Full and brilliant in her white glory. And I…I would be ready. Ready to hunt. Ready to lift my head and bray at the moon.

Ready to feed.

Ready to kill.

"Come on, guv!" The grinning, boyish, good-looking mug of an old childhood friend of mine shouted over the din, "You've suddenly lost a bit of color there. Like you've seen a ghost."

The hard slap of a hand on the shoulder made me grunt as a smile played across my lips. A foaming glass of cold beer slid to a halt on the scarred, battered tabletop in front of me. The chair beside me kicked back, and Mick O'Bannon slid into the chair and grinned at me. We were drinking tonight. Just the two old friends out for a night of drinks and jokes. This was our first stop.

The noisy pub was called Blackfriars, and it was brimming with bodies. Nubile young nymphs dressed to catch the wandering eyes of the lovelorn. Old men in for a draft or two before edging home to the wife and kids. Whores and ladies of the night in to warm their tired worn bodies with a little heat and maybe lucky enough to pick up a trick or two. Young males prime in their health and strength. With leering grins on fuzzy cheeks and a glass of cold beer in a hand as they scouted out their next conquests.

Food.

That's what they all were. Food to someone like me. Someone who worked the night's lonely streets and stalked their unsuspecting prey with consummate skill. Food. Even through the layers of cigarette and cigar smoke, the myriad of perfumes and colognes masking the body scents of the vain, the strong odor of hard liquors—through it all I could smell the true scent. The scent that made my mouth water and my soul ache. That strong, earthy, salty aroma of life.

I could hear them as well. Rhythmically. Pulsating. Ever present; magnified a hundred times with the bodies numerous around me. No. Not their talking. Not the inane speech and mindless banter of children trying to act like adults. Far more primordial, this sound. Like drums this sound was to my ears. Music martial and endless.

The thumping of heart beats muffled slightly within the chest of their hosts. Constant. Hypnotic. Stimulating. Almost…erotic.

"Hey, Roman. Take a look who just walked in."

Through the milling crowd and low-hanging clouds of tobacco smoke I saw him. The pub's door closed behind him, and he stood leaning against the door and eyeing the crowd. Searching the place for someone in particular. Detective Ivan Walker. Wearing his ever-present wrinkled black raincoat with hands stuffed in the pockets and a sardonic sneer painted across his thin lips. A big man who moved—for a human—amazingly smooth and agile.

Our eyes met. And the ever-present sneer on his lips widened.

"Mick, need a rain check tonight, buddy. I believe our friend wants to talk business with me. Let's do this sometime next week. Okay?"

Mick glanced at the approaching Ivan and then, frowning, glanced at me and nodded as he lifted himself out of his chair. Mick was a good friend. A good man. But the law and him had had their unpleasant disagreements over the years. Many of those disagreements coming from my old friend, Ivan Walker.

"Hello, Roman. Out with the boys tonight, are you. Been hitting the bars? Maybe like one over on Harrow Road about an hour ago?"

"Why do you want to know?"

"Roman," the angelic-faced cop sighed, the sigh of a tired man who worked a thankless job for hours unending, and sank into the recently vacated chair beside me. "We need to talk."

Odd.

Odd to hear the melancholic, even riveting, howl of feral dogs lifting their voices up to the white orb of a three-quarter moon. A moon partially hidden by low clouds scudding along in front of an approaching storm.

Odd to hear such music in the city. Such strange, beautiful music.

Odd.

Scattered across several city blocks, their sweet notes came to our ears. Surrounding us. Approaching us. Making several of the uniformed officers surrounding the body lying on the cold, wet sidewalk glance at each other apprehensively and then look over their shoulders in a kind of nervous twitch. The voice of one dog would lift its voice up into the darkness. Soon followed by another directly opposite of the first. And then another. And another. By the time the first dog sang his notes again, it was obvious he was appreciably closer.

Everyone seemed nervous. Even my old pal Ivan. He had reason to be.

Lying at his feet on the sidewalk were the remains of what once had been a man. But no longer. The man's throat had been ripped out. His chest had been shredded to ribbons by razor-sharp talons long and powerful. Eviscerated. Clothes ripped from his body and scatted around the corpse in bloody rags. One shoe sitting upright on the sidewalk about five yards away. Lonely. Surreal. Dramatic.

Looking down at the body, I knew what—who—had committed this foul deed. Someone who hunted in the night. Someone who had a taste for human flesh. Someone…like me. And I could see it in Ivan's eyes. The way he was looking at me. The way his jaw was set. The way his lips twisted to one side of his face. The way he kept his hands in the pockets of his raincoat.

"Who was he?"

"Denton Colbert," the big detective answered quietly. "Lives around the corner in a second-story flat. Was coming home from work. Stopped in a pub about a block away to have a couple of brewskies."

"Was he someone I should know?"

"Not really. As far as we can tell, he was just a steel worker down in the shipyard. No one special. None that we know of. For now."

Far to the north the first rumble of thunder. A storm was coming. The clouds were getting thicker. The night darker. The feral dogs…louder. I glanced at the uniform officers and smiled. Their nervous twitching had upped a notch or two. The pack of dogs seemed to be growing. New voices were being heard. Hungry voices.

"Roman, let's talk," Ivan said quietly, grabbing my arm and steering me away from the group of officers huddled around the body. "I know your condition is…shall we say…insatiable. But as long as you kept, you know, munching on the scum of the earth I didn't…"

"Ivan, it wasn't me. Promise. My—condition, as you call it—hasn't affected me for at least a month. Besides, this was a fresh kill. Maybe a couple of hours ago. I've got witnesses, maybe a dozen of them, who can place me at the bar at that time. People who know me. They'll tell you I never left the place."

Walker glanced over his shoulder at the body and the men standing around it and then back at me. A frown the size of the Channel painted on his lips.

"Another one of you? You fucking gotta be kidding me."

I stared at the man I've known for years. Worked with on a number of cases. An old friend. I called him friend. Yet…my condition, the approaching full moon…was affecting me. My senses were heightened. I could smell him. Smell his blood. Heard the soft thump, thump, thump of his carotid artery in his neck pulsating. My mouth was salivating. My teeth…ached to sink into warm flesh.

"Listen, Ivan. Whoever it was of my kind who did this is an old, old creature. Someone who's mastered his ability to change his shape. He doesn't need a full moon. That means this creature is very smart. Very sure of himself. And he's going to strike again. I'd say in a couple of days."

"When the moon is full," Ivan whispered.

"Yes. So your problem is twofold. First you've got to find out if this is a random act. Was this bloke just unlucky and happened to be at the wrong place at the wrong time? Or is something else going on?"

"And my next problem?"

"You've got to figure out a way to let me finish it. And I'll finish it for you, old buddy. Can't have this kind of thing going on in my bailiwick. This city is only big enough for one of us. And I plan to be that one."

"Yeah, okay." My friend grunted and ran a hand over his lips as he nodded, his frown not receding in the least. "The second part I can handle easier than the first part. Especially if I have only two days to find out everything I can about our victim. But I'll get it done. I'll get it done."

"And Ivan," I said, turning to walk away and looking over my shoulder,

"make sure you and your men are nowhere nearby when things come to a head. I can't promise you there won't be collateral damage otherwise."

The following morning, after a storm filled with lightning and fury ripped through the city with vengeance, the sun came out and adorned a sky painted in light cerulean blue. I got up, brewed some strong black coffee, drank about six cups, then stepped out of my flat and walked to the corner drugstore to buy a paper.

I hate the sun.

I used to love it. But now I detest it. That yellow orb of burning insistence. Enveloping me in a light I cannot shake. Filling me with memories of sins passed. With memories of what once had been. Of impulses I could no longer control. Nor wanted to. Hiding behind a pair of shades as dark as a welder's hood, I walked to the drugstore and kept my mouth shut. Buying a paper and another cup of coffee, I moved to one side and sat down at a table and glanced at the front page.

Jury Foreman for the Wilson Trial Slaughtered

With interest mounting, I read on.

Denton Colbert, the foreman who led the jury in the infamous Wilson trial to an 'innocent of all charges' verdic was found dead last night on a sidewalk in the Berkshire neighborhood.

Colbert, 43, was the one who convinced his fellow jurors the defended, Edward Wilson, was innocent of all charges. Wilson, a notorious gambler, con artist, thief, and alleged murderer, was arrested three months ago for supposedly murdering a young girl named Genevieve Gibbons in a brutal fit of jealous rage. The District Attorney's office thought they had a firm case against Wilson after finding a numberof articles belonging to Wilson in Gibbons' apartment. The most telling item of all the silk tie used by the murderer to strangle his victim and then bind the body on a bed before ripping her throat out and eviscerating the body.

Wilson walked out of the court house amidst a sea of yelling reporters, the flash of camera bulbs, and a large crowd protesting the verdict. Saying nothing, Wilson disappeared into the back seat of a waiting Rolls Royce and...

Lowering the paper, I stared out of one of the drugstore's large plate glass windows absently. In the bright sun people moved in a constant flow of flesh and bone, each in their own world bent on getting somewhere and not caring about who...or what... was near. Deep down in my subconscious I felt the clock ticking away. A little over thirty hours before the full moon. Before feeding. I felt the deep ache in my bones, that itchy feeling in my arms and shoulders. I knew what was coming. Waited for it to explode into reality. Made no effort to resist.

But my immediate thoughts dwelled on something else. Something mentioned in the news article. Genevieve Gibbons died from her throat being ripped out and her body eviscerated. That word again. Eviscerated. A bloody word. Vivid in detail and imagination. A cornucopia of grim sensory delight.

Visions of a body lying in the middle of blood-soaked bed sheets came to mind. Of an apartment ripped to pieces. Of claw marks…long and etched deep into the woodwork…to be found in numerous places. Glancing at the paper again, I read the article two more times. And frowned. There was no mention of claw marks. What did that mean? None were found? Or were the police reluctant to mention them in their reports?

The cell phone riding in my slacks began sounding off as I reached for my coffee.

"Did you see this morning's headlines?"

"Yes. Now we know why he was selected."

"I don't follow," Ivan grunted, sounding confused. "You think this Colbert fellow was murdered by a werewolf because of something to do with bringing an innocent verdict back in Edward Wilson's trial? Why would Wilson want to kill Colbert? The dead guy saved Wilson's ass from hanging."

"I didn't say Wilson had anything to do with it, buddy. But I'll bet you a month's salary our dead guy was ripped to pieces because of the verdict he delivered."

"Hell, Roman. You don't make enough money to buy a fucking jelly roll with your coffee, much less make a bet with me," Walker chuckled over the phone. "But what's the connection?"

"The woman. Genevieve Gibbons."

"Gibbons! What the hell?! How did you come up with that cockamamie idea?"

"Ivan, did you read the article?" I asked.

"Well...no. I just glanced at it."

"Read the article. Pay attention to how she died. See if that kinda jingles any bells for you. Now tell me, who was the lead investigator in this case?" I asked.

"Bill Vanderbilt. You know him. He's over in the Bridesdale Precinct."

Sure. I knew him. Good man. Honest and perceptive. A stickler for details. His reports would be thorough. If there were any claw marks in the woodwork, he would have mentioned them. If...

"I need to see Bill's case reports, Ivan. All of them. And a list of jurors. Can you get them for me?"

"Sure, Roman. Sure. Give me a few hours to collect them.. Let's meet at a pub for some lunch later today. I'll have them by then."

"Jimmy's," I said, nodding. "'bout twelve-thirty."

"Right. See you then."

Flipping the phone closed, I dripped it in my slacks pockets again and reached for the coffee. The sun's bright light exploded through the window in front of me. The goddamn sunlight.

God. I hated the sunlight with a deep, deep passion.

Ivan was eating a triple burger soaked in cheese and dripping in blood-red ketchup, the red of the ketchup brilliantly luminescent every time I glanced up to look. Around us the crowd pressed in close. People were dropping in to grab their carry-outs and leaving. The door to the pub kept opening and closing in a staccato of bright sunlight and loud city traffic.

The crowd who stayed and tried to grab a fast bite was heavy and just as loud. Sitting at a small table tucked away in a corner, I sat with legs crossed and the thick case file Detective Sergeant

Bill Vanderbilt had assembled and read with interest. On the table in front of me was a tall bottle of Smirnoff vodka and an empty glass filled with ice. My lunch. Thirty-some-odd hours before the full moon, it was all I could stomach.

Ivan ate and drank his beer, and I studied the photos of the crime scene of Genevieve's apartment. And the more I looked and read the reports, the more I became angry.

"Ivan, what the hell? There are photos missing. And roughly five pages of notes."

"I know." My friend nodded, lifting a hand to his lips and burping quietly. "District Attorney Radcliff removed them."

"Radcliff? Why would Radcliff remove pages and photos of an investigation from an official file?"

"He said he couldn't prosecute something like this if the evidence Bill found in the apartment remained. He said the public wouldn't...couldn't...believe such a theory as Bill was suggesting. There was no such thing as werewolves! I heard he really ripped into Bill in his office. Called him a fool. Told him he was sloppy. Said he was going to reassign him to some patrol beat down on the wharves if he didn't expunge some material."

"How do you know all of this?"

"Bill heard about our little murder last night. Gave me a call about an hour ago. We had a little chat about it. Compared the crime photos. Made some notes."

"And?" I asked expectantly.

"You were right," he answered, burping softly at the same time and frowning. "Damn onions. I love onions. But they don't love me..."

"Ivan!"

"Oh...right. You were right. Deep claw marks on the wooden headboard of the bed. Some on the bedroom door frame. The kind of marks...you know...someone like, uh, you might leave behind. And here's the interesting thing. The claw marks? From a left-handed werewolf. Left-handed."

"I'm not left-handed," I said quietly.

"I know." My friend nodded, a hand holding his lips and burping again. "Damn. Come about four o'clock tonight, and I'll be farting onions. You can bet on it!"

I had to smile. There had been many a night when, as a cop and as Ivan's partner sitting in a car on a stake out, his farts became a subject of long debates. Pouring a still jolt of vodka over the ice in the glass in front of me, I sat the bottle down and reached for the glass.

"Alcohol doesn't, you know, dull your senses?"

"This close to a full moon, I'm getting so pumped up alcohol actually cuts the edge off a little bit," I answered, flicking the wrist and shooting the cold vodka down my throat. "But remember. You said you didn't want to know about my condition."

"I know I know," my friend nodded, but looking at me oddly. "Still…I'm curious, you know? I mean, how long have I known you, Roman? Ten…fifteen years? We were partners for how long? Five? Six?"

"Seven," I answered, filling my shot glass with vodka again.

"Yeah, seven. Good times. Lots of laughs. Saved my ass more times than I can count. And then you get bitten by that…by that thing. And poof! Here we are. I'm still human, and you're a fucking werewolf. A killer. And here I am sitting at the table with you and talking to you like we were still on the force together. Like we were still friends."

I turned my head and looked at Ivan's rugged features for a few moments.

"We are still friends, aren't we?"

A grin spread across the handsome face of my old friend. A wide smirk of sardonic pleasure. A kid's mischievous sneer of pure bravado.

"Every minute of every day—except for about three days of the month. Give or take a day or two."

I grinned and lifted the glass of vodka up in the air. Ivan lifted his bottle of beer, and we clinked glass in a silent salute before drinking. Setting our drinks back on the table, I turned my attention back toward the thick report.

"Who was Genevieve Gibbons?" I asked.

"Ha! Get this," Ivan barked, his sardonic lips widening. "She was a court reporter. Worked most of the big felony cases. Good at her job. Friendly. Pretty. Flirtatious, some would say. Rumor has it she and D.A. Radcliff had a thing going on together."

"So Radcliff had a personal interest in nailing Edward Wilson as the murderer."

"Oh, God, yes! Wanted to pin the murder on Wilson so bad he could taste it. Been trying to take down Edward Wilson for years. Years! Thought he had him dead to rights with that blue silk tie he used to tie her up. A one-off kind of tie. Made exclusively for Wilson."

"Did Wilson know the woman?"

Ivan's wicked grin widened as he silently nodded his head and rolled his eyes merrily. But then he sat back in his chair, and his face became serious.

"But where does this Colbert guy come in? He was just the foreman on the jury. Didn't know Edward Wilson from some bumpkins at the bus station. Didn't know Genevieve Gibbons. But he dies in the same fashion as Gibbons. From a left-handed werewolf."

I eyed my old friend and then looked down at the file folder on my knee. Rifling through a few pages, I found the sheet I was looking for. The list of names of those who served on the jury.

"Alphabetical order, just as you ordered, old hairy one," Ivan said, smiling like a kid again. "Say, this is fun. Working like this with you. It's like old times!"

"Yeah, fun," I repeated, shaking my head and almost smiling.

Denton Colbert's name was the first name on the list. Underneath his name was one Mary Collins. Beside her name was her address. She lived cross town close to Vinland Park. A big swath of raw country that bordered the county. Filled with trees, underbrush, and wild animals. Including packs of feral dogs. And other creatures.

"I know that look on your face, Roman." Ivan grunted, sitting back in his chair and reaching for his beer. "What are you thinking?"

"I'm thinking maybe we have our killer's next target," I said as I gazed at the name. "We'll know in the next few hours."

"Want me to send some boys over to her place and keep an eye on her?"

"No. You and your men stay away. I'll handle it. If I'm wrong on this, no harm done. We'll think of something else. If I'm right…"

"I know. If the moon is full, you're going to go ape shit. And neither me, nor my men, want to be around when that happens."

No, my friend. You really didn't want to be anywhere near me when the moon burned bright and full in the heavens dark and lonely.

A heavy mist covered the streets and stuck to the buildings with a wet clinging desperation. And growing. With each passing minute, the mist increased in its size and thickness. The night air was still. Very still. The City's streets were devoid of traffic. Parked cars lined the curbs on both sides of the streets. Dripping wet from the mist and partially hidden. The sidewalks devoid of pedestrians. Empty and desolate; aching with a kind of dread it knew was coming.

Above me low, dark clouds flew across the face of the three-quarters moon. Odd that clouds raced across the sky driven by forces unseen. Yet here standing in the darkness across the street from Mary Collins' apartment, the air was as still as a mummy's breath.

I felt the caressing touch of the moon's soft yellow beams burrowing into the flesh of my neck and shoulders. I felt the fire of the coming fury burning in my blood. My senses—all—even now augmented a hundred-fold. My hearing so intense I heard the soft mumbling of those sitting in their apartments behind solid walls from across the street. Thinking themselves safe and secure from the ravages of the night.

The fools.

In my soul I knew he would come. In my blood I could feel the growing presence of a predator coming to ravage Mary Collins. The night before the full moon—before the time when I too would be like him—he was coming with fangs sharp and long. With claws as wicked as the edge of razors. He would come on two legs, a black figure thick in the fur of a wolf with the aromatic whiff of wild insanity about it. He would come. The lust to kill and to feast on the carcass of his victim blinding him. Forcing him to take chances he would otherwise refrain from doing.

But most frightening of all, he would be an old werewolf. A cunning creature long in experience and survival. So old he could turn into his alternate ego whenever he wished without the benefit of the full moon. Old and cunning. Capable of rational thought even as the fury gripped his soul and pulsed through his arteries.

I half turned and glanced up at the three-quarter moon. And frowned. There would be no way I could challenge this creature tonight. No single mortal could. The creature would be too fast, too strong, too vicious to confront. Even if I could get close. Get close to deliver the death blow—it would be impossible to do. The creature would break me in two as if I was but a spent match ready to be thrown away. My strength. My agility. My resolve nothing compared to the wolf's.

Faintly in the distance the first voice of a feral dog lifting the first lonely notes of a song toward the moon. Followed by another. And another. With the sounds lifting into the night sky came the first gentle touch of a cold, almost frigid, breeze. The white mist hugging the ground begin to stir. To twist. To contort as if it was in pain and agony. Hugging close to the deep shadows of the building beside me, I stood motionless and waited for the creature to appear.

When he came, it was in a way I least expected.

From behind me.

I caught the aroma of thick, wet fur. Of a huge wild animal. And the strong, salty aroma of fresh blood. I heard the sharp, distinct snort of animal. Felt the explosion of his breath across my neck. And…I heard his thoughts.

Behind you, Roman. Look behind you.

I gripped the panic trying to sweep across my senses and held it firmly in check as I turned around. It came out of the darkness of the alley, out of the swirling mist of the night. Tall and massive and foul-smelling. The largest creature I had ever seen. It towered over me by a good two feet. Powerful shoulders rippled with immense strength as it moved toward me. Arms muscled and as thick as ships' mooring cables hanging in a relaxed fashion down its sides. Walking on legs bulging and massive.

Out of the darkness and mist it strode toward me. Confident. Arrogant. Completely in control. I could smell the first blood covering the sharp snout. I saw fresh blood smeared across the fur on his chest. It had just killed. It had feasted on its victim. And now it was towering over me. Its giant, luminescent dark eyes boring into mine with a kind of amused insolence.

I know who you are, Roman. I know what you have become. I saw you the other night standing with Detective Walker. I caught the whiff of your...sickness. Think you can defeat me, young cur? Think you can destroy me?

A hand, claws pulled in and hidden, swept out of the night and caught me on the side of my face. A blow powerful enough to lift me off my feet and hurl me out of the alley and into the street. I bounced off the hood of a car and rolled off its fender, dazed and semiconscious.

I know you've taken Mary Collins and whisked her off to someplace safe. I know you think you can trap me and run me to ground. Fool!

A hand swept out, grabbed me around the chest, and violently jerked me up into the air. Another blow, a ringing slap across the side of my face, sent me flying again through the air. I don't remember hitting the hard pavement. I was barely conscious. Blinking several times in blinding pain, I stared up at the three-quarter moon and waited for the creature to come closer. As I knew it would. With an effort, I slid a hand underneath the trench coat I was wearing and wrapped fingers around the one weapon I knew could kill a werewolf.

Ha, ha, ha! So you think you can kill me with a stake of pure silver driven into my heart, Roman! Ha, ha, ha! So pathetic! So meaningless!

Powerful hands hoisted me into the air. The werewolf's face—his fangs bloody and stained—close to mine. I struggled to pull out the foot-long silver spike from underneath my trench coat. But the wolf pressed his fingers into the flesh and bone of my right shoulder so hard I screamed in pain and froze in agony. Fury gripped the creature's mind. I could feel it. I could hear it. He laughed and started pulling me closer to him. He was going to finish it. Going to rip my throat out. Drink my blood. And there was nothing I could do to stop him.

Boom!

The shattering explosion of a 9mm pistol ripped through

the night. *Boom!* A second gun went off right behind the first. I heard the wolf grunt in pain. I felt the creature pull back his dripping fangs from my throat and turn his head to look at the new threat approaching him. Vaguely I heard voices—Ivan Walker's voice—screaming at his men to follow him and to shoot at the thing holding me up in the air. The grip on my shoulder relaxed just enough for me to move my arm. Out came the silver spike still gripped in my hand. Deep into the creature's left shoulder I buried the spike. Not a killing blow—but a painful one. A very painful one.

The creature dropped me to the pavement, staggered back a couple of steps, gripping its wounded shoulder as it turned to howl in rage at the approaching police officers. Fangs bared, crouching, it roared in fury again at the terrified men and then turned to me and snapped at me viciously. I rolled away just in time. Fangs ripped into the back of my trench coat, just missing my flesh, and shredded it to pieces before I rolled free.

And then it was gone. It fled. Fled with unbelievable speed and agility. As I lay on the wet pavement of the street, vaguely away of a dozen or so beams of flashlights dancing in the night air above me, I looked at the three-quarter moon and thought about the terror I had just faced.

And the terror I had become.

"That was a close one," Ivan, handing me a bottle of beer and belching. "Jesus. That thing was big."

We were standing in the kitchen of my flat. The flat top of a small bar separated us. Taking a long drag from the bottle, wincing from the pain pulsating in my skull, I eyed my friend angrily.

"I told you I didn't want you and your boys around. Now what do you do? Your men saw a werewolf. What are they going to say in their reports? What are you going to say?"

Ivan looked at me, gave me that smirking grin he was famous for, and shrugged.

"Hungry. You hungry? I'm hungry," he said, pulling away from the bar and walking over to the flat's refrigerator. "Got anything to make a sandwich in here? Or do you just stack the fridge with bottles and bottles of Type O-positive blood?"

"I'm a werewolf, Ivan. Not a vampire," I said dryly.

He pulled the fridge's door open and bent down to peer in. Throwing out an 'Ah!' he grabbed a dish of cold quiche and stood up and turned to look at me with surprise clearly written on his face.

"Quiche? A beer-drinking, boozer-turned-werewolf has-been like you still eats quiche? I'm shocked, Roman. Shocked!"

The big man dug around for a fork in the kitchen cabinets until he found one and then walked back to the bar, forking out big chunks of the quiche and hungrily devouring it. I grinned and lifted the bottle of beer in my hand for another pull.

"Now, to answer your question, my friend. Who the hell at headquarters is going to believe there are werewolves? Who? Anyone who'd write something like that in their report, and I guarantee you they'll be six months in a loony bin doing psychiatric workups. With strange-looking doctors with unpronounceable German names holding syringes attached to long needles in their hands at their bedside looking down at them. You're safe, Roman. None of the men are going to say a damn thing."

"But that means our killer is safe as well," I said, lowering the bottle of beer.

"No, not really. I said the men wouldn't mention anything in their reports about a werewolf. But there's nothing said about reporting nabbing a crazed psychopath serial killer who thought he was a werewolf! Our best chance to find this fucker rests on your shoulders, Roman. I suggest we find him as soon as possible. Before he kills again."

"When he was talking to me I could see he had already feasted on a kill. Someone is dead, Ivan. The questions is…who?"

"I got men on it asking around," Ivan said, burping, walking over to the kitchen sink and rinsing out the now empty dish in some water and setting it down in the sink. "He didn't kill Mary Collins. He didn't attack the third person on the jury list. That we know. So maybe your theory needs a little tinkering. Maybe we're walking down a wrong path."

Maybe.

Maybe not.

Frowning, I glanced at my watch. The full moon was coming. The Fury. The Blood Lust. Only a few hours away. And my old friend was still close to me. Hanging around and putting himself in danger. Somehow I had to get rid of him. Without actually getting rid of him.

"There's a connection with the trial, our dead juror, Edward Wilson, the district attorney, and the dead girl Genevieve Gibbons. My gut tells me there is. All you've got to do is find it, Ivan. Find it before tonight."

Ivan lifted his head and looked at me and frowned. I knew he was reading me. Reading the tone of my voice. Reading the way I was looking at him. And he was picking up the vibes. I could see it in his face.

"He's coming for you, isn't he?"

I said nothing for a moment or two and then quietly nodded.

"He's wounded," the big detective went on. "You poked a silver stake into his shoulder. He's hurting and pissed. He knows you're not going to give up looking for him—and now he knows the police are looking for him as well. Tonight's a full moon. So the two of you are going to tangle."

"Find out the connection that links all the dead people together, Ivan. Find out before the moon comes out. If not… don't think about coming over and interfering. Ivan, I mean it. When I change I can't guarantee your safety. I could turn on you just as fast as I will with this thing. Get in the middle of this and you could be very dead. Understand?"

Ivan gave me a grin and slapped me fondly on my shoulder as he walked past and reached for his raincoat. Sliding into it, he plopped on his head the battered old fedora he was fond of and headed for the flat's entrance.

"I'll give you a call if we find anything, Roman."

I nodded and watched my friend open the entrance door and then pause and turn to look at me.

"And Roman, watch your back. This thing isn't going to underestimate your talents again."

And neither would I, I thought to myself. *Neither would I.*

I used to be a cop. A good cop. Recommendations and commendations littering a wall in my office. Now I was a private investigator. Self-employed. Poorly paid. Working from one paycheck to the next most months trying to pay the bills. But the same kind of work. The same methodology. I knew how to track down a suspect. I knew how to observe a suspect without being observed. I decided to track down and observe District Attorney Anthony Radcliff.

Anthony Radcliff was forty-five years old and handsome. Tall, fit; looked like a freshly minted C-note in his custom-tailored, conservatively cut three-piece suits. Teeth as white as a billiard's cue ball, wavy black hair—the guy made women's hearts just go a-flutter every time he batted his deep brown eyes at them.

He also was vain. He knew he was good-looking. He knew he could make a woman, almost any woman, fall in love with him. He married the right person by using this talent. His wife of five years was worth about sixty million dollars. Old money, with family connections running through the halls of power that ran deep. Just the wife a rising star like Anthony Radcliff needed to make his mark in the world.

The problem was, after a little digging and a couple of hours watching him come and go out of his office, it became obvious this man wasn't the killer of Genevieve Gibbons or Denton Colbert. Nor was he the creature who so smugly assumed he was going to devour me the night before. The first nail in that coffin came when I found out early in my snooping that Anthony Radcliff was giving a lecture in a class on Criminal Intent at the local university in the time frame I was fighting for my life. Yeah. Anthony Radcliff, in his spare time, was an assistant professor at the university.

The second piece of evidence which convinced me he was innocent was staged by me. I paid a friend I knew a couple of twenties to accidentally bump into Radcliff's left shoulder as the man left the restaurant where he usually had lunch. The eatery was only a couple of blocks down from City Hall, and everyone knew Radcliff visited the place daily. My friend was young and pretty. Just the person to bump into a guy like Radcliff without rousing too much attention.

Radcliff reacted just like any Lothario would act. She bounced off Radcliff's left shoulder and began apologizing profusely. Radcliff assured her there was no harm done and inside five minutes was stuffing the name and phone number of my friend in a vest pocket and whistling gaily as he started walking back to his office. Free of pain. Completely intact. Devoid of any injury.

Damn.

I tailed him back to City Hall and stood just behind him in the elevator as we rode up to the sixteenth floor and to his office. I followed him out of the elevator and watched him walk down the polished marble floor of the hall toward his office and disappear behind a door. And then I walked over to a battered, scarred-looking wooden bench hugging a hall wall and sat and threw a leg over the other and stared at the wall opposite me.

If Radcliff wasn't our killer, who was? Glancing at my watch, I almost grinned in grim delight. Eight hours until the moon came out full and bright. Eight hours before I turned into the monster I knew I was. And wanted to be.

I stepped into District Attorney's Anthony Radcliff's outer office and walked quietly up to the smiling receptionist sitting behind a large desk of filled with empty space. One or two people were sitting in chairs on either side of me, reading magazines patiently as they waited for turn to see the anointed savior. At the sides of their chairs were heavy-looking briefcases. On their faces was patient indifference at what they were looking at in their hands.

The DA's outer office was big, spacious, Spartan furnished and completely lifeless. The smiling face of the receptionist in front of me was a trained, emotionless mask developed over years facing innumerable idiots who wanted to see her employer. I knew the odds of me seeing Anthony Radcliff would be normally stacked against me by a factor of ten. Anthony Radcliff was a busy man. An important man. He didn't have time to see a simple-minded private investigator like me. But I knew he would see me.

"Good afternoon, sir. How can we help you today?" The receptionist's voice was soft and sweet. And lifeless.

"I need to see Mr. Radcliff. Now. It is a matter of life and death."

"I'm sorry. But District Attorney Radcliff…."

"Here," I said, pushing a hand out with my business card between finger and thumb toward her. "Read the note I wrote on the back. That should convince him I should be seen immediately."

Her pretty smile almost failed her. Her set face of painted perfection almost cracked. Reluctantly she reached up with a dainty hand and took the card and glanced at it. She read the front of the card and didn't bat an eye. Flipping it over, she read what I had scrawled in ink—and almost fell out of her chair. The plastic smile disappeared. The perfect paint on her face actually cracked. Color drained from her face so rapidly I thought she was going to roll out the chair and flop on the thick carpet of the floor, unconscious.

She read the back of the card a second and third time and then came to her feet. There was fury in her eyes. A vein in the middle of her forehead was visibly pulsating. She tried to say something but couldn't. The words stuck in her throat. The only thing she could do was point to an empty seat before turning and stomping down a carpeted hall to the right of her, looking as if she was a Mongol raider about to slit someone's throat.

Grinning, I turned and walked toward the chair pointed out to me and started to sit down. As I did, the cell phone inside a coat pocket chimed up.

"Roman," Ivan's voice came into my ears. Firm. Hard. Filled with anger. "We found our newest victim. Ripped to pieces like the others."

"Who?"

"Edward Wilson. Lying in a bathtub full of blood in his apartment. This doesn't make sense! We need to talk. Where are you?"

The receptionist reappeared, saw me talking on the phone, folded her arms angrily in front of her as one tiny foot began making a tapping sound of furious anger on the soft carpet.

"Busy, old buddy. I'm really busy at the moment," I said,

smiling warmly up into the face of the young girl. "I'll call you back in a few minutes."

Without a word she turned on a heel and started striding furiously down the hall toward the inner sanctum of the D.A.'s office. I followed meekly, making sure I didn't make a sound. The girl looked like a wound-up spring about to pop off and kill someone. Grinning, I knew who that person would be.

Anthony Radcliff stood in the open doorway of his office and he didn't look happy. Sans his suit coat, just a vest and a white shirt underneath it, the knot of his tie pulled down a notch or two, the guy was still a handsome rogue to look at. He saw me, recognized me, frowned more severely. Angrily he turned and waved me into his office before disappearing.

"Close the door behind you!"

It wasn't a request. It was a snarling lunge at my throat. A curt command from a furious creature about to tear into a simpleton. I grinned and quietly closed the door behind me.

"Who the hell do you think you are, Dalton? And what's this shit you wrote on the back of this card: 'I know you killed your girlfriend, Genevieve!' How dare you accuse me of adultery! How dare you accuse me of murder! I'll yank your P.I.'s license for this, you fucking idiot! I'll sue you for slander! I'll…."

I waited until he ran out of air. He screamed. He roared. He threatened. He threw his arms around angrily. He turned about three shades of purple. His eyes threatened to pop out of their eye sockets. But eventually he ran out of air. When he did, I looked up and spoke four words very quietly.

"Edward Wilson is dead."

He froze. Blinked his eyes a dozen or more times at me. The purple hues faded from his face. Dropping his hands to his side, he stood and stared at me. I went on softly.

"Genevieve Gibbons is dead. Denton Colbert is dead. And

now Edward Wilson is dead. Murdered. All had their throats ripped out. All turned into bloody strips of meat. When the papers and news shows get hold of the story about Wilson lying in a bathtub filled with his own blood, they're going to go ape-shit crazy. And when they tie each name to the Wilson case you lost in court the other day…"

"Shit!" the D.A. hissed angrily. "Shit, fuck, shit, shit, shit!"

"Precisely," I nodded, hearing his frustration…and fear…and grinning. "They'll be knocking on your door any minute now."

He turned on a heel and stomped back to his desk. He pulled out a drawer and a big bottle of Scotch materialized in his hand. Turning around, he found two clean glasses in a large cabinet behind his desk. Plopping cubes of ice in both, he poured stiff drinks for the two of us. Grabbing his, he tilted his head toward the other and half drained his glass before I could grab mine.

"How the hell are you tied up in this case?"

"Let's say I'm working for a certain client interested in finding the murderer of Genevieve Gibbons," I said, almost truthfully.

"What the hell do you want from me?"

"Tell me who had a fling with Genevieve. I heard she liked men."

"Ha! That's a fucking understatement! Liked men? She devoured them! She consumed them! She had this insatiable sex drive that simply couldn't be stopped. She went through men like I go through socks in a week's time."

For a moment or two he glared at me in anger, and then slowly the expression changed. It went from rock-hard fury to a grinning Cheshire cat. He was still grinning after pouring himself another drink and looking up at me.

"She was a tigress in bed. Did things that'd just blow your mind. Didn't ask for any commitments. Didn't make any threats.

Didn't want any expensive gifts. She just wanted men. Lots of men. But for a guy like me? Hell. She was perfect!"

"How many others you know of?"

"Here in City Hall? Dozens. Maybe more. She was a very, very popular girl, Dalton. Very popular."

"Any messy entanglements? Sticky situations? Anyone threaten to do her harm?"

"Sure. Mostly younger men. Young lawyers. The guards. Maybe a judge. But nothing serious. She'd tell you up front what she wanted. Made it clear she had no desire to get married or have a long-lasting relationship. She just liked sex. Period."

I sipped the booze I was holding in the glass. Expensive stuff. Good stuff. The two of us drinking booze in his office. Just the two of us. Behind me through the closed office door, the telephones began to erupt like Vesuvius erupting unexpectedly. I saw Radcliff glance at the door and then back at me. That worried look was in his eyes again.

"Tell me about some of the messier affairs. Who were they, and how did she end them?"

It didn't take long. All it took was getting Radcliff to talk. He was a good talker. Had an ear for gossip—as all good trial lawyers do. Three names came up immediately. And when one name came was mentioned, I smiled. I knew I had him. Knew who the killer was. Knew the old werewolf who hid in sheep's clothing.

Now all I had to do was trap him.

When five o'clock rolled around, I followed my newest suspect home. Stayed well back from him—downwind from him—just to be careful. An old werewolf like this one hiding in the midst of his food chain was a wary, cautious creature. His senses much more acute than a normal human's. That's why I stayed downwind from him. I didn't want him to get a whiff of my scent.

He knew my scent. If he caught it while he was in City Hall, or driving home, it would tip him off.

I did notice how he moved. Noticed how he favored and protected his left shoulder. He had full use of the arm. It moved freely. But it hurt him when he did move it. I saw him wince a few times as he moved down into the underground parking garage and opened the door to his car.

He lived in an old section of town filled with every expensive old houses. Big shade trees masked the sun. Old brick streets, in immaculate condition, twisted and turned through very quiet neighborhoods. Deep lawns, professionally maintained, lined the curbs of the streets. It was the last place you would think a werewolf would reside. But it was exactly the place a cagey old creature like this would select. I almost found myself admiring the man's acumen and bravado.

When he pulled into his garage and the big garage door rolled down, cutting him off from the rest of the world, I put the car into Park and reached for my cell phone. Ivan voice's exploded in my ear immediately.

"Where the hell are you?"

"Listen, I know who we're looking for. I'm sitting watching his house now."

"Who is it?"

I told him—and I thought I heard the phone in Ivan's hands clatter to the floor. When he came back on, his voice was quiet and subdued.

"You gotta be shitting me. Do you know what you're saying? We can't arrest this guy! Not without solid, unbreakable, absolute fucking proof. How you going to provide that, Roman?"

"Get some men on it," I answered. "Starting asking around. Talk to the D.A. He was the one who tipped me off. But listen carefully, ole buddy. I'm going to confront him tonight. But I'm not going to kill him. You need to arrest him and bring him to trial."

"Arrest a fucking werewolf! Are you crazy?"

"Not a werewolf, Ivan. A murderer. If I can get him to revert back to human form by the time you and your men get here, it'll all work out perfectly. But the timing is everything. You've got to get here on the dot. Not a second off either way. Understand?"

"On the dot," my old friend repeated cautiously. "But what about you and your...uh...condition? Are you going to be there when I arrive? All hairy and fangy and all?"

"Probably," I answered, worried. "But I won't do anything to you. I promise."

"Is this the same kind of promise you gave when you promised you'd pay back that fifty bucks you owe me? Or is this the kind of promise you promised me when you said you couldn't make any promises about how you handled yourself when you went ape shit. By the way, I'm still waiting for that fifty, thank you."

"Ivan! Just goddamn be here on time!"

"Gotcha. What time you want me there?"

I told him the plan. Of course I was making it up as I talked to him. But it was a plan. It could work—might work—if everything went perfectly. But that's it about plans. Most of the time they don't work exactly like you planned them to work.

"Any questions?" I asked finally.

"One," he grunted for a reply. "Silver kills a werewolf, right?"

"Right. Through the heart. Like a vampire with a wooden stake. But silver. As pure of silver as you can get."

"Can silver bullets work?"

"Maybe," I said, frowning. "But one or two won't do the trick. Even if you did plug him in the heart. There's got to be a certain physical amount of silver. What the hell are you thinking, Ivan?"

"A back-up plan. I'm thinking we need a back-up plan just in case your cockamamie plan doesn't pan out. Which, you know Roman, usually don't."

"Bring guns, then. Lots of guns filled with lots of silver-tipped bullets."

"Oh, don't worry about that, pal. Don't worry about that!"

Ivan hung up and left me sitting in the car and getting worried. Worried about the plan I had just hatched up. Worried about how I was going to control myself once I turned. Worried about what the hell my friend was plotting in that beady little brain of his.

What the hell was Ivan planning?

The moon, bright and full, would rise out of the east around 11:37 p.m. A full moon. A huge orb that would fill one-eighth of the entire horizon as it began to peek over the trees and houses of this quiet neighborhood. Brilliantly yellow white. Brilliantly alluring. Compelling. Bringing with it the burning desire to change. To revert to the fanged savage that lived in me.

Filling me with a madness compelling me to hunt my prey. To kill and ravage him bathed in moonbeams golden and then to lift my blood-stained fangs and snout high to the night air, lifting arms to the goddess above, and sing my victory song to her. I could feel that burning desire—that narcotic longing—building in me. Wanting it to plunge me in a state of ecstasy.

All I had to do was figure out a way to survive until 11:37 p.m.

Sitting in my car across the street from the house of my rival, I felt confident I had followed him home sight unseen. But as twilight built up and then suddenly plunged into the night's deep wickedness, I began to tense. Began to get jittery. The monster I was going to kill was an old, experienced creature of the night.

A very old and experienced creature of the night. I felt confident I could defeat this creature. I was younger. Possibly stronger. Possibly faster. Certainly motivated.

At the same time, a part of me was asking if perhaps I was too confident, too sure of myself. A nagging voice deep in me whispering to me that perhaps I was underestimating my foe's cunning. My foe's strength. His speed.

I should have listened to this small voice deep within the darkest recesses of my mind.

"Good evening, Roman."

The voice! A real voice! Not a telepathic voice only I could hear. But a real voice! Soft and sounding amused—and coming from behind and to the left of me! Coming to me perhaps not more than three or four feet away! I was jolted upright violently like a mental patient being administered electro-shock therapy in the car seat. It was like a fist in the solar plexus. I couldn't breathe. I couldn't focus my eyes. All I could do was turn my head around and stare at the creature standing behind me.

The man had not made one iota of noise approaching the car. Not one iota of sound.

I threw the car door open and leapt out into the night. I knew what time it was. It was 11:30. Just seven minutes before the moon would come rising out of the horizon in all her blazing glory. Seven minutes before I would turn into a monster. Seven long minutes of terror-filled eternity.

"Good evening, Judge Henry," I said as I confronted the man I knew who was the killer of three innocent people.

He stood facing me with a thin smile of controlled amusement on his lips. Hovering around him was an arrogance of assured lethality. A menacing quiet of complete command of the situation. He was a tall man with a massive shock of unruly white hair and bushy white eyebrows. A strong chin. A razor-straight noise. Thin, dressed in blue jeans and a long-sleeved cotton cowboy shirt. He stood facing me with arms grasped behind his back, leaning on one leg and looking as if he was a guest at an outdoor barbecue in someone's backyard.

He was here to kill me. And he wanted me to know he was going to kill me. But first he wanted to savor the situation. To relish seeing the fear mount in my eyes. To relish seeing me collapse in fear over my coming demise. Knowing…knowing then even if I lived long enough for the goddess moon to release the monster in me it would be too late.

Much to my surprise, a sardonic smile played across my lips and I felt suddenly calm and at peace. The voice of the goddess was beginning to whisper…

"You know, Roman, this was all for you. All of it. The three deaths. The elaborate ruse to get you to help your friend Ivan Walker. All of it. I knew you would come. I knew you couldn't say no to your friend. I knew the monster in you would want to track down the monster that is me. And not to my surprise… here you are."

I glanced toward the east expectantly. Vaguely in the night sky I could see the first glow of the moon. Just moments away. Only a few more minutes. If I could keep him talking, if I could stimulate his arrogance and keep him talking, I might have a chance. A fighting chance to survive.

"Those you killed meant nothing to you? Genevieve Gibbons meant nothing to you?"

A soft chuckle escaped the judge's lips as he unclasped his hands and allowed them to fall to his sides casually.

"Not in the least. Nor this Denton Colbert. Certainly not Edward Wilson. They were just the Judas goats needed to draw out my prey. You, Roman. You were the one I was interested in all the time."

"Me?" I asked, backing up involuntarily as the tall man started slowly walking toward me. "What have I done to warrant such an active interest in me?"

"Oh, you know the answer to that, Roman," the judge answered softly, a malevolent smile of dark pleasure stretching his lips back threateningly. "We werewolves are territorial. We can't abide sharing our hunting grounds with another of our kind. Several months ago I caught of whiff of your scent, my dear boy. A powerful scent of a young, freshly turned werewolf. It took some time. Some quiet inquiries. Some tracking in the night around the places I suspected where you hunted. But I found you."

He kept moving toward me slowly. Purposefully. I kept backing up. Stepping away from my car. Moving into the middle of the street. Moving into the intersection. Into a space where I knew the full light of the moon would soon engulf me like some narcotic elixir. And he allowed me to move in that direction. Actually herding me expertly into the residential intersection as if he wanted me to embrace the goddess fully and unencumbered.

In the darkness I heard the monster in front of me laugh softly.

"So you killed Genevieve Gibbons, Denton Colbert, and Edward Wilson. All three just to pull me into some diabolical trap. Is that it, Judge Henry?"

"I killed them all just to get you here, tonight, under a full moon, Roman Dalton. I confess it freely. I confess, my dear boy. I am the one who murdered the three of them. But do you think my confession is ever going to be heard in a court of law? Do you actually believe I'm unaware of what you and your friend are trying to accomplish? After I kill you, whom do you think my hunger will feast on next? Yes. Yes. First you. And then your friend Ivan Walker. He is coming here soon, is he not? Coming alone?"

The moon!

The first beams of a full moon slipped over the upper rim of the quiet neighborhood's trees and swept in a burning hormonal fury across my face! Rage! A roaring in the ears! A surge deep within me. Pain! Exhilaration! Terror! A lust for life! A lust for killing! The pounding of a thousand drums in my head! The surge of unbelievable fury and strength in one flooding…overwhelming deluge!

The two of us—simultaneously—converted into our feral states in the blink of an eye! Fur, fangs, monstrous shapes! Both of us crashing into each other in the full fury of each wanting to kill the other. Claws long and sharp ripping at each other. Fangs aching for the taste of blood snapping at each other's throats. We fought in the intersection of a quiet residential neighborhood unbeknownst to those who lived their quiet, mundane lives in their quiet, mundane homes which surrounded us.

A deadly macabre dance of death. A violent fugue of maleficent fury—each of us trying mightily to rip the other's throat from their neck and suck their blood from their jugular vein.

But somewhere in the fight—somewhere down deep inside me—I know I could not defeat this creature. He was too strong. Too powerful. Too fast. And far, far more cunning. In a blind rage I threw a powerful blow straight into the shoulder I knew was still tender from the wound I gave it the other night. The creature barked in pain in my ear and staggered somewhat. But his eyes filled with his own brand of fury, and he lunged at me—grabbing me by my arms—and lifted me high over his head and threw me from him as if I was nothing but a child's toy being discarded by a petulant child! I flew through the night air a good thirty feet before crashing against the tall sliver of a street light and slamming my head against the pole's unforgiving steel.

I was stunned. Momentarily knocked out. I tried to rise—came up to one knee and tried to stand. But I was too hurt—too weak. Powerful hands gripped me lifted me again into the air. Again I felt myself flying through the night air and suddenly crashing onto the hood of my parked car.

Fool! A whelp like you actually thought he could defeat someone like me? Well, not in this lifetime, Roman Dalton! Not in this lifetime!

I heard the man's heavy breathing and his sense of triumph in my head. I could taste on my lips his desire to taste my blood on his. I knew I was about to die. Yet I wasn't going to die meekly. I would go down fighting. Fighting to my last dying breath.

Summoning all my strength, I slipped off the hood of the car and landed on my feet in front of the automobile's grille and headlights. Gripping the heavy chrome bumper of the car, I ripped it from its brackets and turned with a fury filling every muscle in me toward my enemy. With the piece of steel in my hands, I gripped it like a baseball bat and swung with all my might at the creature. Just underneath its left armpit the steel bit deep into the creature's ribcage. It grunted—bent over in pain—and staggered back three or four steps. I leapt at him, ducked under a swinging strike of his right claws sweeping out to rake across my face. Swinging again with the steel in hands, I bent low and swung for the creature's right kneecap.

I thought I heard bones snapping like match sticks. It seemed to collapse to the street, its mind filling my mind with blinding pain. Pain…and then a fury so powerful, so intense, so primordial words cannot describe it. A hand swept out of the night and ripped the steel bumper from my hands. And then it slammed the weapon across the side of my face. My vision left me. My knees buckled. I vaguely remember falling toward the pavement yet feeling as if I was on a raft adrift in a vast, open sea.

Faintly…very faintly…I thought I heard the staccato barking of something going *poppopoppoppoppop* in one long continuous squeal of noise. And then…nothing.

When I opened my eyes I became aware of three things immediately. First, I stared up into the darkness of my flat's bedroom ceiling. Secondly, I became aware of the soft, luxurious feeling of lying in my own bed. And thirdly…I became aware that I could not move—neither my arms nor my feet.

Looking down I saw leather straps, four of them, tightly binding my arms to my sides. Thick leather straps with heavy steel buckles holding them tightly in its grasp. More straps of the same description clasped my legs together. I could not move. I was barely able to breathe.

I was no longer the raging monster I had so recently became.

In the darkness beside the bed I heard my old friend chuckling in amusement. And then his voice came out of the darkness, dry and sardonic.

"Jesus, you're one heavy bastard when you're all furry and fangy-like, Roman. I damn near got a hernia dragging your fat ass into the van and hiding you before the boys came roaring in with lights flashing and sirens screaming."

"The judge? The confession?"

"Dead. And recorded. In that order," the answer floated to me softly in the darkness. "Took three fully loaded Mac 10s filled with silver bullets to bring his ass down. He didn't go down until the last Mac 10 emptied its ammo clip in him. The bastard."

"You sure he's dead?"

"He's dead. He turned back into human form the moment he hit the pavement. The three Mac 10s punched a hole in his chest the size of a dinner plate. He's gone. And you and your little secret are still safe, ol' buddy. But do me a favor. Don't ask me to go hunting werewolves again. I think I shit in my pants the other night killing this thing. I'm not too keen on doing something like that again."

I took a deep breath, closed my eyes, and smiled. In the darkness, lying in my own bed with heavy straps wrapped around my arms, chest, and legs, it almost felt…safe. The first time I felt like that in a long, long time.

"Listen, you ain't furry anymore, so I'm gonna take the straps off. You feeling strong enough to sit up and share a bottle of Scotch with me?"

"Yeah, Scotch sounds wonderful about now."

A bottle of good Scotch shared with a good friend in the darkness of my warm, stuffy bedroom. The best, I suspected, that I could hope for given the situation I now had to live with for the rest of my life.

The clinking of glasses. The jingle of ice. The smell of the Scotch. And another day of living.

————

B.R. Stateham is a sixty-two-year-old dreamer who has been writing about dark things for more than forty-five years. Dark noir, dark fantasy, dark hard-boiled detectives—the things that go bump in the night. In other words, the author may be old. But he's still a kid at heart.

FEAR THE NIGHT

Julia Madeleine

I GOT THE CALL WHILE I WAS AT DUFFY'S, late on a Saturday night. I was keeping company with Jim Beam, my vision just beginning to blur in a comfortable sort of way. I'd talked to this guy twice before on the phone. And both times I'd told him I couldn't help. But he was stubborn. Either that, or he figured if he kept asking me the same damn question in various ways, I'd eventually give him an answer he liked. This time his voice seemed more frantic, a hint of genuine fear present at the edge of each word.

"I've got money. That's not a problem," he said in his thick French accent, panting over the line as if he were being chased down a dark alley by a pack of brain-sucking ghouls. "Whatever you want, Roman. And all your expenses too. Flight, hotel, a car. Please—"

"Like I said before, I don't know if I can help you." I wanted to get this guy off the phone so I could focus on my drinking.

"Two hundred thousand. And another hundred thousand bonus if you're successful."

"Listen here, George, is it?" I said, staring at a solitary ice cube floating in my glass like a miniature full moon in a galaxy of alcohol.

"Gino, it's Gino."

I let out a breath, thinking suddenly that it might be a good idea to get out of town for a while. Maybe a change of scenery was precisely what I needed. Shake the cobwebs loose from my mind. It's a funny thing with distance, it gives you perspective somehow. And three hundred grand if I'm successful? Who couldn't be bought for that kind of loot? I was no saint. Besides, I had nothing to lose.

"I can't make any promises, like I said before. There's no guarantee, you understand," I said.

"I have faith in you. My cousin says you're the best. And that's what this is going to take."

Gino booked me a flight and emailed me the ticket information. I had another drink and packed a suitcase. Early the next morning, I headed out of The City on a plane heading to Quebec city. I had a sandwich on the flight and a few shots to quell the tremor in my hands. I stretched out my long legs as much as I could into the aisle and then enjoyed a nap, in spite of the screaming babies on board, which sounded just like pterodactyls.

I was a little concerned with the pending full moon in two more nights, but I'd learned to control things, prepare for the beast that took over my being on those occasions. Before I left, my former partner Walker, who still had my back, checked on Google Earth for the nearest wooded area to where my hotel was located. There I'd be able to hunt a coyote or a deer, satisfy the blood lust that would undoubtedly overcome me. Nobody had to get hurt. Unless, of course, they needed hurting.

When my plane landed at the airport, I spied my name written in black marker on a piece of cardboard, held in front of a little balding man. He was dressed in a suit that was undertaker black, and a fuchsia tie.

"Roman Dalton," I said and flicked his sign with my finger. "That would be me."

The puckered lines on his forehead smoothed out as he gazed up at me with wet eyes, searching my face as if just the sight of me would bring him the relief he so eagerly sought.

"Bonjour," he said, shaking my hand, his smile widening. He flashed unnaturally white teeth. "Thank you for coming."

There was an unexpected strength in his grip for someone who looked like they were fast approaching their golden years. I felt suddenly sorry for him and what he must be going through. It's not that I hadn't felt compassion when he first told me his story. I'm not heartless. Just self-absorbed these days with my own problems. Besides, I really wasn't interested in getting involved in the beginning. Not until he'd upped his offer so much that I couldn't refuse. But now that I was in, the seriousness of the situation dawned on me uncomfortably, like a backpack full of cinderblocks loaded squarely onto my shoulders. Sweat prickled in my pits. I needed a drink.

He led me through the airport, asking perfunctory questions about my flight, if I'd ever been to Quebec, did I speak French. I knew enough of the language to get me around, not that I could carry on a conversation. But I could order in a restaurant, ask for directions, that sort of thing.

A stretch black limo was waiting for us outside. When the driver reached for my bag, I stepped back, insisting that I'd keep it with me. Being an old cop, my trust level was pretty much nonexistent, even with my luggage, which I hadn't checked but packed in a carry-on.

"So give me the low-down. As much info as you have," I said to Gino as we sat in the back of the car, enveloped in the air-conditioned chill.

The car pulled out onto the road and merged with the late afternoon traffic. Swollen clouds the colour of beaten flesh sat low on the horizon, concealing the hot August sun. Ozzy's "Bark at the Moon" came on the radio, and the corners of my mouth lifted. But the driver switched the station, stopping on a cheerful-sounding song which seemed entirely wrong in that moment.

"My daughter Alana was always a good girl," Gino began, looking down at his hands folded in his lap. "She was such a joy to her mother and me. She was happy, good in school, never in any trouble. But then things took a bad turn and Alana...she didn't handle it well."

He looked out the tinted window for a moment, turned his gaze back down to his hands, and continued. "She was just sixteen when her mother died. Alana didn't recover from it. She went crazy, doing drugs, drinking, running around all hours of the night. I tried so hard. Believe me I tried, but...teenage girls, you know?"

He gave a nervous chuckle. I nodded encouragingly. The light in his eyes faded as he said, "I didn't just lose my wife that day, Roman. I lost my daughter, too."

"What leads do the police have?" I asked.

"The police?" He laughed and shifted in his seat. "On their list of important things to investigate, Alana's at the bottom. They simply don't care. She's expendable in their books."

"When was the last time you talked to your daughter, Gino?"

"Six months ago. She called me from that place where she was working, said she wanted to come home. I told her I'd come get her but she said no, she had purchased a bus ticket and was on her way. So I went to the station to meet her. But she wasn't there. They said she never got on the bus." He swiped a hand over his face and sniffed. "I've been up there to that place countless times, sitting in the parking lot, walking the streets looking for her. It's closed down now. The story is that the girls were doing more than just stripping and the town shut them down. But that's not the truth. There's rumours. People saying things about a massacre at the club and the town's trying to cover it up."

The car slowed as traffic clogged on the highway, construction bringing things to a near halt. Gino took something from the inside pocket of his jacket and handed it to me.

"This is a picture of her," he said.

I gazed at a school photo of a pretty, fresh-faced girl, all the certainty of a bright future reflected in her large blue eyes. She had a heart-shaped face, framed by blonde hair. I was struck by how young and innocent she appeared, with a small upturned nose, and dimples in both cheeks.

"There's something going on up there in that town," Gino said. "People know things, and they're afraid to talk. They board their windows up at night. There was one man who told me some things. Told me about the massacre at the club. At least ten people. Dancers mostly. Then he turned up dead himself. I tried to go to the cops. They don't take me seriously. Think I'm just some old man who's lost his marbles."

Gino blew out a shaky breath and looked at me with grave eyes. "All I want, Roman, is to find out what happened to my little girl. If she's alive or otherwise. I need to know—I just need to know what happened to her."

I was dropped off at a Delta. There was a rental car for me in the underground parking. Gino handed me the keys, along with a map to where I could find the Club l'Emotion, some photographs of the place, and a fat envelope.

"What I promised you," he said sadly.

I tucked the envelope inside my bag, and told him I'd set out after I'd checked in and gotten a bite to eat. We shook hands, and I watched him walk out through the glass doors to his limo, thinking, *I hope I'm not going to disappoint this man.*

I lubricated my mind with a couple of drinks in the lobby bar, ate half a bowl of over-salted peanuts, and watched a baseball game on the row of flat screens. Then I headed out in the rental car.

L'Isle-Verte was the name of the town, and it was about a two-hour drive from Quebec city. I arrived with the sun low in a coral sky. A near full moon rose above, the colour of bleached bone. I felt the beast begin to shift inside me, coil through my veins. The hairs on my limbs prickled. Like a drug addict, I loathed it and I longed for it.

I gassed up the car in town, not that it needed it. It was an excuse to talk the old guy who worked there in the station. I showed him Alana's picture, asked about the former strip club. He shook his head, actually shooed me away as if I were a mosquito. The doorlock clicked behind me as I exited, and the man turned a "*ferme*" sign in the window. Talk about putting out the welcome mat. Maybe a good laxative would help cure that personality disorder of his.

I stopped at a diner in town for a meal. I flirted with the middle-aged waitress as she poured my coffee, enticing smiles from her, and even a blush in her chubby cheeks. She giggled at my bad French. When I asked her about l'Emotion, her smile melted and her eyes darkened. She looked around nervously and then in her French accent she whispered, "We don't talk about that place."

"I'm looking for a girl who used to work there," I said and pulled the picture of Alana from my pocket. "An underage girl. I'd appreciate anything you could tell me. If you've seen her before."

She gazed at the picture and then gave me a level stare, blatant fear in her eyes. She shook her head and said, "I don't know anything."

She moved away. It was obvious she had information she wasn't sharing. Later, when she placed the bill on the table, I placed a hand over hers and squeezed. "Anything you can tell me about her, if you've seen her."

She sighed, pressed her lips together, and said, "She used to come in here. All the girls did. For breakfast. She was a nice girl, sweet, you know? Not like the others."

She peered around for a moment and then in a hushed voice said, "I heard she was killed inside that place. All the girls were. Murdered. None of the locals dare go there, even though it's an antique store now. Only out-of-towners. We don't even leave our houses at night anymore. People fear the night around here."

"Murdered by whom?"

"Monsters," she said and hurried away.

I recognized the white structure from the collection of photographs Gino had given me, its faded pink and white sign announcing "Bar l'Emotion Danseuses" still swinging from the front of the building. Scattered around the parking lot was a collection of random junk; dining room chairs, various pieces of bedroom furniture, bicycles, a red bathtub, doors and windows. Gino had told me the place had been turned into a junk store. It was still strange to see the original sign for the strip club on the building.

I parked and stepped out of the car, gravel crunching underneath my Doc Martins. The setting sun bled a deep shade of pink, making the ropy clouds appear like intestines on the horizon. A warm breeze kicked up dust from the field in back of the building, a stretch of dark land that reached to the banks of the St. Lawrence River. The iridescent light of the moon reflected over the water in the distance, turning it silver.

A foul odour on the breeze caught in the back of my throat like a fishhook, making me gag. I'd know that smell anywhere.

It was the sickening stench of a thousand putrid cesspools. Excrement, decay, death, and old blood.

Zombies.

Fucking zombies. I spit on the ground in disgust. I loathed zombies more than anything.

A man came out of the front door of the building. He was tough-looking, compact like a pit bull, maybe in his early thirties. He looked at me without smiling, a dead stare in his eyes.

"*Je suis ferme*," he said, in a flat voice that was more of a grunt.

"Sorry, just a quick look, then. I won't be long," I said, and offered a half smile.

He picked up a chair lying on its side and nodded without looking at me.

"*Merci*," I said, and took a careful step inside the building. It was dark inside, shadows filling the corners, the evening sun straining weak as a whisper through the grimy window in the front of the place. The stench of zombies was stronger in here. It closed in around me, folding over me like a slimy membrane. Not only could I smell them lurking in the dark, watching me, I could feel them. Every fibre of my body, every cell and nerve was attuned to their frequency.

Fucking goddamn zombies. It was crawling with them.

The place still had the original setup from when it was a strip club. The stage was there along the far wall, now piled with a variety of crap from old mattresses to baby paraphernalia, a disco ball suspended overhead. The bar was intact, complete with stools and dusty champagne glasses hanging from the ceiling. And the private booths still had sheers in front of them as if waiting for customers and gyrating dancers to fill them. I heard something move in the shadows. A thump and then something falling, like a coin on the floor. I stared hard into the darkness, sensed movement. Slowly, I stepped backward and then kept backing up. When I was at the front door, I looked down and to the right. I laid eyes on an axe leaning up against the wall. It looked like there was blood on the blade. I turned and walked out. In the parking lot, the man was piling stuff into the back of a pickup, a cigarette stuck out from the corner of his mouth.

He didn't look up at me as I approached. When I tried to talk, ask questions about the place, he got inside his truck, flicked his cigarette at my feet out the window, and hit the gas, leaving me in a cloud of dust. People certainly were friendly in this town. I got back inside my car and left. I would wait until dark and then come back. In fact, I'd wait until the next night when the moon was full to come back. Then I'd get down to business.

I drove back to my hotel, lost myself inside of a bottle of whiskey, and fell into a fitful sleep, battling creatures in my dreams. The next day I woke around noon. I inhaled a plate of bacon and eggs in the hotel's restaurant, drank three cups of coffee to clear the mood of the fever-dream images that sat heavy inside of me. Then I headed back to Isle-Vert and the zombie's paradise set up inside the former strip club.

I walked around the quaint little country town, had an ice cream cone, checked out a few local shops. I bought a flashlight in a hardware store, and waited until sundown. If Alana was still there, lurking inside that club with the rest of the ghouls, I would find her.

The moon was icy white in a purple sky, stippling the tops of the trees with frosted light, gleaming dully on the rural mailboxes jutting out at the side of the highway. It shone on the tarmac like a stage light, waiting for me. In a vacant lot a few yards up from l'Emotion, I parked the car and stepped out into the warm night air, fragrant with cow manure and clover. The sound of crickets was shrill in my ears as if they were screaming. I had the flashlight, flanked at my thigh. I walked up the deserted highway, my senses in overdrive. I could feel the beast emerging, twisting inside me. My bones ached and my flesh burned with the familiar agony coming upon me. My body felt like a freakish machine on these nights. Suddenly I thought of my former partner Walker, wishing I would have been able to bring him with me for backup. I longed for the days when we had worked the job together. Being a private eye was a lonely business.

The moon rose behind me, waxing full, and pressing into me. The stench of the ghouls reached my nostrils as I neared the building. I felt myself break out in a sweat. The bastards. Hateful fucking things they were, the undead. I saw a darkened mass—a figure—move in the shadows near the building. It lurched along awkwardly and then rounded the back.

Fucking zombies. I spit on the ground.

I stood in the shadows outside, listening to the crashing sounds from within the bar. What were they doing in there? Bumping around and tripping over all the junk inside? I heard yelling. A man. Had they found themselves a late-night snack and dragged him back to share? Without waiting any further, I took a run at the front door and gave it a high kick, knocking it off its hinges. The agony inside my body was cresting. My muscles began to spasm and stretch painfully. I moved inside the building, panting, my heart slamming against my ribs. I shone the flashlight around me, its white beam landing on the hideous faces of the creatures that lurked in the dark.

The pit bull–looking man from yesterday who wouldn't talk to me was standing in the middle of the room, swinging an axe at the zombies. The arm of one of them went flying in the air as he chopped it clean off. The zombie let out a moan as if it had actually felt it. She was a tall one, matted red hair hanging down around her shoulders in clumps. She wore a sheer babydoll with lacy panties that might have once been pink but were now so soiled with blood and filth they were nothing more than rags hanging in tatters from her rotting frame. I could see knee-high red patent leather boots on her feet. To think this thing could have actually once been a living breathing woman who enticed men to part with their hard-earned money with just the bat of an eyelash…it was too much to fathom.

Pit bull–man took another swing at her and she lurched backward, falling into the shadows. Another zombie came at him, another female in a long red dress, torn and filthy, her black hair so matted it looked like bad '80s rock star hair. She managed to latch onto the man's shoulder, but he shook her loose and swung the axe at her, just missing her midsection as she took a clumsy step backward. She fell against some junk on a table. Glass crashed, shattering on the floor. Zombies were stupid, slow things. Killing them wasn't too difficult.

A sound behind me. I swung around with the flashlight, the beam landing on a face straight out of a nightmare. And in spite of the decay, greenish skin sliding off her skull, I recognized the upturned nose, the large eyes, the heart-shaped face, the blonde hair now like filthy straw.

"Alana?" I said.

She twitched her head and stared at me as if a fragment of a long-dead memory had come to her. She was a tiny thing, more petite than I'd expected. She wore a threadbare blue bikini with a smattering of silver sparkles now worn off or hanging in shreds of fabric. What used to be her right breast was exposed but was little more than drooping putrid flesh sliding off, like a blackened banana long past its expiry. Her skin was a sickening greenish-grey tone, rotted through in places. And on her feet, a pair of spike-heeled lace-up boots that may have been white at one time.

Pain seized my guts and shot through me. My bones twisted. My spine arched, and all my muscles swelled and lengthened. I felt my ribcage crack open, the flesh on my body ripple with the skin that gave way to the thick fur of the beast emerging from within me.

Alana studied me as the transformation took place before her eyes, reacting to it as if there was still some shred of life left in her, a vestige of humanity. Was it possible she knew what she had become? Was there still memory left in her brain of her former life?

I could think no more with the agony seizing me. I let out a scream as the beast took over, and it became a roar that issued from my fanged mouth. The bass sound shook the floor beneath the taloned paws that had become my feet. The sound of my bones popping filled the air. Razor-sharp nails ripped through my flesh as the bones in my hands cracked and twisted into massive claws. I dropped the flashlight and it landed into a pile of crap next to me, its beam shooting up at a forty-five-degree angle.

I felt the familiar thrill of the enormous power in my limbs, all of my senses alive and exaggerated. My tail twitched and swished around my hind legs. My ears scraped the ceiling. I drew in a breath, and a thunderous howl burst from my lungs.

Alana hissed and jerked forward. I took a swipe at her, my claws shredding the rotten flesh on her chest. Another swipe, and her head shot into the air before me like a volleyball, tumbling repulsively through the beam from the flashlight before crashing into the darkness. Her body dropped to the floor with a thud. A mirror leaning against the wall fell on top of her and smashed.

I turned on my hind legs when I saw the other zombies lurching toward me. The man with the axe was staring at me, open-mouthed. The smell of urine filled my nostrils as he pissed himself. He let out a cry, dropped his axe, then turned and ran into the darkness.

I lifted one of the zombies in the air, spun it around as easy as a stick, and snapped it in two. The breaking of bone like gunshots.

One high-heel shoe flew off as I tossed the corpse away. Another stripper zombie came at me. I swiped at its head, chopping it from the neck as easy as popping the stem from a cherry, and hurled the head at the wall. My fangs tore the arm off another one. I couldn't help notice that it was wearing silver hoop earrings that flashed in the light beam, its mass of tangled hair held back in a ponytail. Taking the severed arm in one of my claws, I used it as a baseball bat to take off its head and watched the glint of the earrings as the head spun through the air. Several more made the mistake of trying to ambush me.

Stupid zombies. God, I hated the fuckers. And stripper zombies? They were the worst. Creepy as all hell in their lingerie and stage outfits. Fucking stripper zombies.

One of them hissed at me, and I gave it a backhand. The head spun a full one-eighty and then popped off. I kicked what remained of its corpse into another two of them, knocking them down like bowling pins. Before they got back to their feet, I clawed at their throats, ripping off their heads. Three more approached me, and I severed their heads all at the same time with one quick swipe of my massive claw. It was a beautiful thing, watching their heads bounce across the room.

I released a roar, looking around for more of the ghouls. Except for the sound of my breath, the place was still. I'd gotten them all. Picking my way through the body parts, I spied the remains of Alana's corpse. Something glinted on one of her fingers. I cocked my head and squinted. It was a ring. An emerald. I pulled it off her finger and clutched it in my paw. Alana was free now. Free to catch a ride on that ghost bus back home to her daddy.

I ran into the night, down into a field, where I stared up at the full moon, bathing me in its frosty light. I released a long, satisfying howl.

Hours later, when the beast receded inside me, I walked back along the highway shivering. I was beat, every fibre of my body spent. Back at my hotel I phoned Gino. I was sitting in the hotel's bar, sipping on Jim Beam Black when Gino pulled up a stool beside me. He looked at me with his sad expectant eyes and I told him the truth about his daughter. I placed the emerald ring on the bar, where it glittered under the lights. I felt my throat close up for a moment as I watched him reach for it. He brought it to his lips and closed his eyes.

"It was her mother's," he said in a whisper.

"Sorry this story doesn't have a happy ending," I said and knocked back the rest of my drink, motioning to the bartender for a refill.

"It does," he said and pressed his lips together. He stood, placed a fat envelope on the bar beside me, and said, "At least for you, Roman."

He thanked me, walked out, and left me thinking about happiness and what that meant. They say money couldn't buy happiness. I glanced down at the end of the bar, where a stunning Asian girl with raven hair was giving me that knowing smile all the working girls had. I toasted her, taking the bait. But then again, I thought, money could buy me a whole hell of lot of pleasure. And that made me very happy indeed.

Julia Madeleine is a thriller writer and tattoo artist living on the outskirts of Toronto with her husband and teenage daughter. She is the author of the novels *No One to Hear You Scream* and *The Truth About Scarlet Rose*. Visit Julia's websites for more information on her writing and art: www.juliamadeleine.com and www.malefictattoos.com.

BACK TO NATURE

Jason Michel

IT IS TIME.

Time to get out of The bloody City.

The nightly lowlifes are still out in force at this early hour. There have been jokes cracked at someone else's expense, heads cracked for money and hearts broken for a quick dose of glandular pleasure. Another night in The City drags itself to bed.

As much as I love the rotting playground where I live, there are times... Yes, there are times.

We pass the streets and back alleys, all dingy grey and rubbish-hued as the sun gingerly pokes its head up, and I realise I need a cigarette. I do not care how long it has been since the last coffin nail, but today ain't the time for quitting anything. Not booze. Not smokes. Not a damn thing.

This is the time for excess. For the mind to go batshit crazy.

To batten down the mental hatches and see myself in all my glory.

Some people go on holiday to burning sun loungers, or spend a week of foot-ache tramping from one old dusty cliché to another, or visit world-famous dens of iniquity to abandon themselves to flesh.

Me? Well, I get back to nature.

The mist rises up from the evergreen forest like the breath of some mossy forgotten god. The sombre outline of the trees is stolen by pale cloud, and for a moment the world vanishes. We have been driving since the early morning, and our bodies and minds are tired. Still, could be worse. Could be dead.

Dead.

Duffy inches his foot down on the accelerator, and I realise that the spliff we smoked ten minutes ago is making my arms cold. All the blood seems to be rushing to my head. My ears are radiators. Duffy's car pulls me down the rain-graced road, and we sit in stoned silence as the hashish floods into our minds for one more buzz, for the road, and I hurtle my way towards a dark place filled with the black light of the beast.

Aren't I just a cheery fucking lycanthrope?

A right hippie howler.

We turn off the main road and onto a dirt track and drive until the track becomes nothing more than a path. Duffy stops the car with a jolt and I grab my bag from the boot. He bites off a little piece of the Moroccan before he chucks me the rest.

And with a wink, he is gone.

The cabin appears exactly the same as every year. Right down to the spider's web over the eaves and that birthmark rust, just-so, on the hinges. My holiday home. A ramshackle shed that from the outside resembles Richard Nixon. You have to see to see it to believe it. This wormrot ex-Presidential shack with its population of window frame–hugging arachnids and mutant silverfish dwelling in its mildewed mattress. I retrieve the key under the eaves, trying ever so delicately not to destroy the ancient web that has made this place its own. I turn it in the lock and push the door open as it scrapes on the floor and lets out a miserable groan of spite. In I go.

That rum old bugger, MacIntyre, must wring his hands with miserly glee every once a year when he sees my number on his phone.

I drop my bags onto the mattress, which, surprisingly, doesn't squirm, and I am overjoyed to find that there is running water flowing from the stiff taps. That never ceases to amaze me. I rinse and fill up the kettle, then check to see if the old weasel has filled up an extra gas bottle. He has! Wonders will never cease. Then I realise that he will probably charge me extra.

Soon the kettle begins its tortured whistle and I put it out of its misery, dashing the hopes of a teabag while I'm at it. I skin up another doob while I'm waiting for the black tea to brew, then pour myself a hot tall one and head out to the front steps.

The forest around me heaves and blinks its recognition, and I stare right back at it. A calm descends upon me, as if the dark-green valley and I are in a post-coital embrace. I breathe in the tingly damp air that provides some relief from the hot and spicy hashish, and the mixture purges me of the city with all its crime, hubris, and civilised obscenity. I begin to feel the animal inside me wake up and stretch. It is clawing and scratching to be given free rein, and tonight is for him.

Catholics have their confession. Others lie on sweaty sheets, hoping night after night to be entered by Christ. Tibetan Buddhists sit on uncomfortable pillows in gaudy temples chanting "Om Mani Padme Hum," feeling secretly superior and thoroughly wasting their time. This is my retreat. Where I let the beast inside roar, wallowing in the moonlight. Just the forest, the wolf, and the moon. A savage trinity. A triptych of blood and noise.

The invisible sun is beginning to set now, somewhere up there in the cold cloudy sky.

They shall be here soon.

Now, here's a moral dilemma for you:

I'm ex-Inspector Lon Chaney, Jr., the P.I. who never kissed ass but can lick his own balls. A man who has spent his life trying to right wrongs, solve crimes, stick up for the little man.

A sleuth.

Lemon Entry, my dear Wolfson.

Involuntarily, I go and get myself a malediction, and I am turned into a creature that commits the most heinous of crimes without discrimination. Men, women, children. Innocent and guilty. They mean nothing to the Wolf. Not when he comes a-knocking. Blood lust is all that matters. That itch that I, the honest if slightly dishevelled law enforcer, experiences in my dreams and in the creaks of nighttime floorboards. That itch is always lurking there, somewhere behind the subconscious ,and you just know it will only get worse if I do not scratch it every now and then. Stands to reason.

"Hand yourself in!"

Not going to happen. Think I want to be prodded and poked by some Frankenstein in his underground laboratory while some military rung-climber thinks up ways of using my curse to kill thousands of people I do not know on a battlefield somewhere in a place that does not have two sticks to rub together to make fire while they cook their camel stew.

"Kill yourself, you devil's spawn!"

I ain't no bad guy, and you are the one yelling for murder. Not me.

Yes, I feel guilty for the deaths of the innocent. Which is why I am here.

See, it ain't that simple at all. There are rules beyond your civilised society. The laws of my kin. The Man-Wolf. If I am in any way to obey those laws, then walking the razor's edge between the dream of mankind and the reality of the beast is my path.

This is the law, and we each and every one cope with it in our own ways.

Coming here to speak to the dead is my terrible penance.

And as I step inside, close the door, and light the oil lamp, I can hear the wind whispering my name.

The bottle of Dark Valentine glugs and shimmers in the lamp light while I pour myself a tiny helper. I drink. And another. And another. And another. Through the haze of pungent smoke and bittersweet whiskey, the memories knock their way into my skull in sharp flashes that make my head hurt. This is the only time that I can remember my crimes. They batter at me in Technicolour. Every gouge and tear and crack of a criminal's ribcage. Every drawing in of the tongue while lapping at a child's warm blood from an open neck wound who should have listened to mummy and not got out of bed to look for her lost puppy. Every chewed heart.

I'm spinning my Colt .38 on the table as the jagged souvenirs come passing through me. Bathing me in their moments of gore. The gun spins faster. Faster. A gentle rumbling of metal on wood. Having them so close. They are there waiting on the other side of the night, waiting like they do every year for our little appointment. They are gathering just beyond the shadows, and the hairs on my arms stand to attention and I take another deep drag on that spliff. Keeping the smoke way down deep. Another deep drag to unlock the doors and usher in my most welcome guests.

The lamp flame begins to dance and spit.

An imprisoned spiteful sprite.

I pour myself another glass, down it, and stand up, swaying through blurred eyes.

My arms open, seemingly by themselves, in a gesture of fearful welcome, and I collapse back into my chair.

And come they do.

At first the wind around the cabin hisses, "*Ddaaaaaaalllltoooooooooooon!*" and I begin to see images, hazy at first, a wild flickering in the corner of my eye.

They are everywhere distorted, tuning in on the spirit of radio.

In the corner the little girl with less than half a neck, her head and strawberry blonde pigtails lolling loosely, thrusts her right hand forward accusingly, and I hear the shrieks of her murder all over again. Behind me one of Ton Ton Philippe's goons takes a swing with the only arm he has left after I had ripped the other one off. The blow sends shivers down my spine. Lying on his back with his lizard entrails split from his stomach, creeping slowly towards me, Wallace Strain, caught between a Moonie and Creature from the Black Latrine, flails his limbs in what seems to be some horrific squawking temper tantrum. Some decrepit homeless geezer takes his last piss once again in the sink while his spine swaying right and left like some ghastly metronome. His insane sloshing gibber. Speaking in tongues. If only he had one left.

And still more come.

A disco abattoir.

They enter to declare my guilt. Pointing and screaming. Thumping their breasts and gnashing their gums. Dragging their spastic dance across my feet. Blurring faces that fall apart in front of my eyes. Cadavers that I have no memory of creating until they pass their hands through me and suddenly I see their deaths, each and every one, and the pressure builds inside my head, and I think that the aneurysm that my ex secretly wished upon me is finally coming to pass. A man can never truly escape the curse of a woman.

The whole cabin is spinning with death. I spin the gun. A scratch-robed chest-scarred hooker and her headless John are fucking in the toilet forever, and a Joey Franco the East-Side Mob Boss is poking at my head with his big dumb chewed-to-the-bone knuckle. I smell a rotten whiff of his aftershave and spin the gun again. The pain and pressure in my skull clamps me down to the chair and I fill my mug up again. Jesus, my hands are shaking as I lift the mug to my lips. The pain slices into my mind. I drop the mug, spilling the contents all over the floor, and from the cupboard comes a hideous giggling.

The moon is rising.

It stirs my blood.

I spin the gun.

The beast howls in the distance.

Somewhere around my id.

I spin the gun.

The phantom freak show continues to spin 'round and around my head.

I try to stand up using the chair.

It is nuzzling its way into my ego.

"STOP!" I shout, feeling a surge of animal energy sobering up my blood.

It is time.

All eye sockets are on me.

This is what they came for.

Now or never.

Before the beast becomes manifest, becomes me.

I grab the .38 off the table and press it hard to my own temple, and through my nausea and dizziness the crescendo builds.

"AAAAAAAAAAAAAGGGGGHHHHHHHHH."

Now.

I pull the trigger.

I am blind.

Deaf.

Dumb.

Senses extinguished.

Memories erased.

I die every full moon.

A dot of me trapped inside this savage body.

I lick my lips and taste the morning dew mixed in with something gamey. Wabbit, I'd wager. I lie there between the pine needles and snowdrops for a time. It is exhausting. The morning after the night before. My feeble body has been stretched and twisted and pushed to its limit. Getting too old for all this. It is getting lighter by the minute, so I drag myself up and look around.

God knows where I am.

Here we go again.

It takes me two hours to make my way down into the bottom of the valley. My bare feet are in tatters, as is my patience. Even my balls got scratched by some cheeky old brambles. Stumbling around the forest cap in hand. Ho hum. Could be worse. Could be…

The road is somewhere around here, I know it. Then I see the smoke. A trickle of translucent grey through the trees. A forest fire? No chance. It is soggier than a van full of Waterboys fans in a monsoon. As I make my careful way through the bushes and scraping the pine bark, I realise that the smoke is coming from a wooden cottage. I can see it way off in the distance. I did not think anybody lived in these woods, and I am damn sure that swine MacIntyre told me that. Why I would believe that scoundrel is beyond me, but this changes everything. I have been coming to let Old Hairy loose precisely because there were no people for miles around. No innocents to kill. Dammit!

Making my way towards the glade, I wonder why someone would want to be here.

Is it someone sick of the city and all its fester?

A holiday getaway?

A hippie commune?

A couple of hundred yards from the door, I kneel down gingerly behind a bush, choosing a decent vantage point for my spying.

The wind carries a sad melody to me.

Singing.

I can hear a sweet voice singing.

Popping my head up, I see a woman. Long raven-black hair, a flowing gown of brown and green. She is sat on the steps of the rustic cottage, combing her hair. By the bloody moon, her hair is long!

I sneak down towards the voice, trying to avoid stubbing my tip-toes on the sharp rocks scattered around, and creep behind a grand old Norwegian spruce. Something catches my eye, and I look up to see thousands upon thousands of spiders' web all tangled up above my head. I gaze around and notice that all the trees around the edge of the glade seemed to be covered in a vast amount of webs. I momentarily think what a fearless woman she must be! Then a shaft of sunlight breaks through the thick stern clouds and rests upon the high branches. The webs become a silver mist above me. The beauty and craft of these sticky creations overwhelms me as the wind gently stirs them. They seem to be moving to the sound of the melody wafting around my head.

"HELLO!?"

I freeze, and my nuts shrivel even smaller and tighter than walnuts.

"Hee-llooo?"

Poking my head out from behind the scratchy bark, I see the woman walking curiously towards me.

"Hi!" I shout back, as friendly as I can. If a bare-assed man covered in cuts and bruises turns up on your doorstep, the least the nudist can do is be polite, don'tcha think?

"Are you okay?"

I can see her face now. She is smiling a pretty one.

"Sort of! *Ummm*…I seem to have lost all my clothes, *he he*! I don't suppose you have a sheet I could wear, do you?"

I wince while I'm speaking.

"Wait here!" she laughs. Without blinking or questioning she runs back to the abode, disappearing inside the shadowy interior. She reappears a minute or so later, holding a bundle in her arms. Coming closer to the tree, she throws the bundle in my direction. A pair of corduroy slacks, a checked shirt, and some moccasins land with a soft thump at my feet. She turns around, and I emerge from behind the tree, grab the clothes, and wrestle with them awkwardly. The slacks are a little large in all the wrong places and the shirt is tight enough to let my chest hairs poke through the gaps between buttons. Finally, I slip on the warm wool moccasins, which pleasantly tickle my feet. I look up to see my saviour facing me. She stares hard through her coy smile.

"Come with me," she says.

She tells me her name is Ariadne. As she spins her story, I

watch her body gracefully move. I do not think I have ever seen a woman move with such elegance. Her hair reaches way down. It almost touches the floor. She was born here, out in the woods, she tells me as she sprinkles some tea leaves into a teapot. She is a widow, she tells me as we sip our tea together. She works with a spinning wheel, buying wool from the local farmers, then creating warm clothes for the winter, which she sells in the local markets. Her husband was a carpenter, as strong as any man. He died in an accident while out collecting wood one day. She does not tell me the details, and I see no need to pry.

"Your husband lost a lot of weight out here, eh?" I say, tugging at the waistband of the slacks, feeling the tight shirt over my chest. Her eyes flash, then widen in understanding.

"Yes." She smiles a smile, neither of joy nor sorrow, but there is something undefined in her green eyes.

"He did. Are you hungry?" she asks.

It is the first question to pass her lips since we entered the immaculate cottage with its strong pine table and homely home-made rugs. There is not a speck of dust. She is quite a housekeeper.

"I could eat a horse," I reply. "Rare."

She giggles.

"Come in to my parlour."

The rest of the day is spent busying around the cottage, and after chopping some wood and lighting a fire I have quite forgotten the madness of the night before and my ritual of Russian Roulette in front of a select group of spooky onlookers. In fact, it is beginning to seem as if I have always been here. Even the memories of a life spent in the raw shadow of experience are fading. I swear, even the clothes fit better.

The evening falls, and I watch her working on the spinning wheel in silence. She throws her long hair behind her as strands fall upon her face and I sip at a honeyed tea. I watch this dark Rapunzel at her work as her fingers tug deftly at the yarn and she begins humming a tune. I close my eyes and lose myself in the silk thread labyrinth of her voice.

"To bed," I hear her coo as her jet black locks caress my check. I am led into her chamber and undressed. I suddenly I want the answer to a question.

"Why are you not afraid of the spiders?"

A strand of her hair touches my breast and she breathes heavily into my ear.

"They create as I do. Why should I fear them?"

She gazes out of window, lost in some reverie.

"They are my children."

I feel that this answer is true is some way and understand. I also feel a connection with nature. A savage link with the moon. She creates while I destroy.

Her hair engulfs me in shadow, and my tired and damaged body is stroked, not by flesh, but by a soft follicle tickle. Even as she mounts me I think of silk.

Eventually we are both brought to climax. I spill into her womb, and I feel the darkness engulfing me in a little death.

My eyes open.

All I see is red.

My head is dizzy and I cannot feel my feet. This is one helluva hangover in a life of too many. My arms and legs are bound tight. Shit. Within a couple of tear-y blinks, my vision starts to clear and I see the earth rising up into the sky. No, the bruising clouds are at my feet.

Upside down.

Shit.

Something small and many legged crawls over my face. I

hear Ariadne's soft cooing above me. I try to move my head but the binding is too tight. Expertly done. A soft curtain of darkness moves into my vision that brushes my face.

"Ariadne!" I cry.

Scared now. Whatever has strung me up must have gotten to her, too.

"Ariadne!"

"Hush, my love. Your name is Roman. Such a strong name. A warrior's name. Are you a warrior, my love?"

Her voice is mesmerising.

How did she know my name?

The voice goes on.

"My warrior. My wolf. You too have had a life as bizarre as mine, my love. I saw it as I bathed in your memories."

The black cascade continues to fall. I blink and suddenly there she is, in front of my face, as upside down as I am. Up close. Her nose almost touches mine.

"What's happening?" I squawk through a dry throat.

"Rejoice! You are going to be a father," she utters.

Her face disappears, to be replaced by coarse hair and a click-clack scuttling sound.

Then I see and my mind goes flippity-flappity.

She is on the ground.

IT.

It is on the ground.

That beautiful head on top of a pale monstrosity. The eight limbs move and dance as the joints click-clack with perverted grace. That skinny thorax with its bulbous child-bearing abdomen. The coarse hairs standing on end. Black and red spots that tell you that the female of the species is far more deadly than the male. A mockery of all that is natural. I feel bile falling downwards into my mouth as I remember the previous night's abandonment and ecstasy. Sex with a demon from an old French grimoire. Sheesh.

Her...

Shakes head

ITS humming starts again, and with that hypnotic chant comes its story:

"Escaped from Hell, I did.

The Lords and Ladies of Cruelty search high and low.

They shall never find Ariadne.

Escaped to be in love, I did.

I found it here, amongst the trees and shadows.

My carpenter loved me and gave me offspring, but die he did.

I wept when he passed and tore strips from my own soul.

But die he had to, for my children to live.

To feed on.

This is a mother's sacrifice.

So it is written and we cannot change.

Now, I have you, my love.

I shall keep you here.

To do your duty.

We are one."

Lost.

I am lost.

Three days have passed, I think. I fall in and out of conscious-ness in a fevered madness. It feeds me on honey, cake, and water three times a day. I am so delirious that most of the time I just chew at the dry sweetness and the mulch eventually falls out of my mouth onto the damp forest floor. After she feeds me, she kisses me on the lips and tells me how happy she is. I try not to retch, as there is nothing left in me and the spasms just hurt. I have managed to convince it to turn me feet downwards, which she did as smoothly as working the thread on the spinning wheel. I am still suspended six feet above the ground, but now my head no longer rests against the jagged broken lower branches. Its already massive belly is now huge and swollen. Things are wriggling and tickling inside it.

Not long now.

It is day five.

Today she comes in human form. Naked. Her belly is the size of a pulsing elephant's skull. She lies down on her back in front of me. She spreads her legs wide and gives birth to hundreds of thousands of tiny eggs. Arachnoid caviare spew from her impossibly stretched gash onto the ripe earth. She purrs her melody throughout the birth. Once they are all steaming in a small rotten hill, she takes them up into her arms piecemeal by piecemeal, effortlessly climbs up the tree and attaches them to my chest, my stomach, my legs. They hang heavy on me, and I find increasingly difficult to breathe.

"Daddy will look after you," she gurgles.

Above me their brothers and sister drop down out of the trees to bid them greeting.

I have given up cursing her.

Night has just fallen, and I awake from a fitful half-sleep. I hear the snap of twigs below me. Some night creature wandering on the off chance for a kill or scavenge. I inhale sharply, feeling the weight on my ribcage. Another snap. Then something gently gently swings my feet. I feel something climbing the tree and tense myself through fear. I hear the deep breathing of effort.

"Knew I'd find you hanging somewhere around here!"

Duffy's whisper scares the shite outta me, yet I start to laugh.

So, you have heard that spider's webs are stronger than steel, right?

Well, Duffy sits on a branch and sets to work on the web with his lock-knife like the champion he is and blunts the fucker within a few cuts. I wriggle like a beheaded worm, but to no avail. I am still stuck fast. He tells me that he has been looking all over the forest since the morning after he dropped me off. It was the smoke that brought him here.

"Get me fuckin' outta here!" I hiss.

"Alright, Peter Parker! Just hang in there."

Now, he is a smug smartass.

"You want a slug of whiskey, matey?" He leans back on the tree and takes hip flask out of his jacket pocket. I try to nod; he understands and places the mouth to my lips and tips. The liquid burns as it goes down, but I stop myself from coughing. Duffy takes a swig and lights himself up a smoke. He inserts it in my mouth and I take a deep old drag, feeling the smoke foul my lungs beautifully. He takes it away for a second, just enough time for me to exhale, then replaces it, and as he does the cherry of the cigarette falls off. It lands on a sticky piece of thread and begins to smoulder. I begin to blow at it and then...

Holy shit.

"Burn it!" I sneer.

"What?"

"Burn the fucking thread!"

Duffy begins to chuckle and slaps himself on the head.

"Just bend your knees when you hit the floor, Tarzan."

"Fuck off!" I grin.

Landing with a thump, I feel the eggs slip off me as gravity works its magic and Duffy's Zippo takes care of most of the web. I am left naked with a couple of burns but nothing too serious.

Duffy has brought some spare clothes. The bastard thinks of everything.

In the distance, the soft purring of Ariadne's (or whatever-the-hell that thing is really called) singing scents the air around us. I thought my falling might have warned it, but it must be so wrapped up in its own twisted form of longing for future motherhood. I almost feel sympathy for it.

Almost.

They say that the way you live can kill you.

Live by the sword, die by the sword.

Well, I wonder what fire does to a demon from the burning pit?

With great care, we make our way towards the cottage. Duffy goes as quiet as a mouse to find something flammable while I peer in through the window. It is sitting at the spinning wheel. She (yes, she) is perfect again and looks so happy. She seems lost in some reverie. I think you could drop a bomb on the whole frigging wooden house and she would not wake up from it. Inside me the beast rages. He claws at my urge for vengeance, pushing it on, forcing it over the edge. A vengeance born out of fear and disgust. A very human revenge.

My hands tighten into fists.

I feel a hard gust of wind at my back. A draught makes the candle light flicker, and I see her smile inside her devilish thoughts. Such a quiet and loving smile. I see her loneliness for what it is. Her need for love. An inhuman love. One we have absolutely no way of comprehending.

And I make a decision, gaze at her her loveliness one last time, and turn around. Behind me, Duffy is sneaking around like some drunken thief. He is holding a can in his hand with liquid sloshing around inside. I walk up to him.

"Petrol," he mouths as he undoes the cap and lets me sniff. The vapour is overpowering for my weak head. He mimics throwing the petrol onto the walls and roof of the log cabin. Waiting for my approval, he nods expectantly.

I shake my head and motion for him to follow me back to the edge of glade.

I've seen too much death recently.

The rank spawn-pile of eggs lies where they were discarded, and I gesture at them.

"Do it," I whisper, and he drenches the result of a lycanthrope and a demon. I wonder idly if they would have been wolf spiders, as he tears a strip of cloth from his shirt. Wiping it over and inside the stubby mouth and neck of the can. Soaking it.

Wolf spiders.

Guess we shall never know.

"Run!" he wheezes, as his Zippo flicks into life and a tiny flame is born that gets larger as it catches and consumes the rag. I turn on my aching heels and hobble as fast as I can manage. Behind me is a WHOOOSHHH and I feel Duffy at my heels. As we pass through the trees, the upper branches seem to be screaming with despair.

A death in the family will do that to you.

As we make a mad scramble up the hill, another sound echoes in the distance.

A howl of parental anguish.

An unholy despair.

Once we get to the top of the hill, it takes us another three hours of tramping blindly around the gigantic nocturnal wood with nothing more but Duffy's luminous compass to guide us. We do not dare use his torch to light our way. But finally reach the road, we do. Every now and then a maniacal squeal floats into earshot, and far off into the distance we can hear something large tearing through the lonesome pines.

A hellspawn who tasted something deep of our experience, and I imagine the madness crashing into Ariadne as when we mere mortals receive a glimpse into their world.

Two hours later, and we climb into Duffy's rust bucket. I have gathered all my belongings from the shed in haste, and the next thing I know we are out on the open road. Duffy chucks me his gear, and I fill up my battered cup with a large Dark Valentine and I skin up a fatty.

We smoke it as the morning sun opens its eyes in the heavens.

The clouds are clearing.

It is going to be a beautiful morning.

"Let's go home," I say, and Duffy winks a nod at me.

———

Jason Michel is the dictator of *Pulp Metal Magazine* and *Pulp Metal Fiction.* He is the author of *And the Streets Screamed Blue Murder!* and *Confessions of a Black Dog.* He lives in France.

BLOOD AND ALCOHOL

Frank Duffy

A LOT OF PEOPLE SAY they know The City. They talk of its geography, of its famous places with their exaggerated antiquity. They talk of its history enshrined in landmarks best forgotten, of peerless do-gooders given statues on tree-lined boulevards, of new buildings replicating past fake glories. These same people like to talk of photographs in books written by men who are merely tourists in this landscape. Even the rats and cockroaches have a better grasp of The City than they. Only those men in bars who speak quietly of jobs done in the darkness of alleyways, their souls turned out for some pocket change like a piece of lint stuck to their faded police badges, really understand The City.

Men who dance on the decaying underbelly to the staccato beat of its nightly violence. Men like Roman Dalton.

This is The City, half-constructed buildings like megalithic arrangements, their roofs sloping precariously to the rotting sewage of the Queen Anne river.

But there is another stench besides that of the river. Blood and alcohol. Men who never plan or know, or feel anything because the alcohol has blanketed them in disgraceful entropy, swaddling them in the firmaments of arbitrary and senseless murders.

Like this man.

Edwin Sturbridge stood on the edge of The City docks, contemplating throwing himself into the waters of the great river, when a flash of light like zinc flaring under a welder's torch caught his eye.

"Aye, nay's well it been now rather than later," he said to Al Leadon, whose sleeping form beside a thick knotted bow rope hid him practically from view of anybody who might happen to walk past. "Perhaps it's like that Yankee film with Jimmy Stewart. Somebody's come to save what's left of me life. Eh?" He glanced down at Al, kicked him, and then pretended he wasn't there.

Edwin was of course referring to *What A Life! Whoops the Angels!*, that perennial Christmas day Hollywood favorite of families up and down the country. Naturally, he hated the movie on account of its condescending faith in human worth.

"Blasted waste of celluloid, if ye's asking me," he snarled.

Al showed no sign of waking from the forty fathoms of drunken sleep he presently inhabited. There would be no discussion tonight to discuss the finer points of moviemaking or angelic interference in ordinary people's lives.

Not that Edwin believed in guardian angels or the afterlife. In his view, which at that moment was enflamed by a half liter of Tennessee Wild Turkey, and a hit of cheap laudanum off one of Song Chi's "Night Ladies" over in Willow Park, anything which hinted at his current incarnation being prolonged once he'd shuffled off this debased and pitiless planet, was just one more magnificently turd-shaped example of yet further irony being heaped upon years of accumulated past ironies.

As his late brother Harry had once said to him, "as the world's most cuckolded sonofabitch you should have clawed your way into your ma's intestinal sack and drowned, rather than supped your weary way out of her poor rotten womb."

Not long after Harry had made another of his acerbic appraisals of his brother "convalescing in our ma's uterus like a swollen cancer," Edwin had stabbed him through the eye with a roasting fork, and buried his dismembered body in a lime pit on the other side of town where he buried most of those people he'd killed.

Edwin wasn't a proficient or even an intelligent murderer. Most of those he'd butchered, garroted, or bludgeoned to death, he'd done so out of some depressing bout of spontaneity.

"Maybe's I should do me brittle-faced wife," he muttered, until that strange light flared again.

Last night it'd been his wife annoying him, her shrill voice detailing her supposed dalliances with several of the regulars down the End Lane public house. A coppers haunt. She knew perfectly well he wasn't going to bother with any of that lot.

There was fog on the river, which pretty much resembled the smog of the industrial chimneys rolling over the clustered rooftops of The City. Not a good night for making out much of anything.

Still, the light sputtered between the bows of two tugs like blocks of rounded cement in the fog. There was somebody there, too, a figure standing behind the light as if directing it to searching him out.

He gave Al another kick, but his drinking buddy merely rolled over so that he was precariously balanced on the edge of the dock, the filthy waters of the river waiting below. Edwin bent down and rolled him off the edge of the dock and watched him hit the water with a muffled splash. He was doing Al a favor. What was a watery grave at the bottom of the river in comparison to the two-bedroom hovel he shared with his common-in-law wife and nine kids?

Al didn't even wake when he sank beneath the water, and it was only then that Edwin realized he was taking such a chance with the narc being not more than fifty feet away, though in the fog they might have been closer than they were.

If he was honest with himself, which was a lot more than people gave him credit for, Edwin felt killing somehow elevated him out of the undignified place life wanted him. But as that strange light turned from a sparkling champagne-white to a luridness the shade of the red light district, the knowledge that he'd probably no more robbed Al wife's of a husband and father than he had a verbal punching bag, was a steadily diminishing second as the light spread out across the buildings on the docks. Some of it slid up the sides of boats, port windows like glassy expressionless faces in its searching gaze, until finally it found him.

Edwin knew not to run. That's what City narc wanted.

"I'm just out's here drinking meself silly." The light maintained its angle, three-quarters of it lighting him up, except his right side, which hovered in shadow, and Edwin felt the incompleteness.

The figure behind the light said something, but the words, mostly unintelligible, were more curiously discomforting than was the autumn cold seeping through his clothes now the booze and the laudanum was wearing off.

Edwin saw there were at least two more figures behind the one holding the light, standing on either side, also faceless against the glare.

"Hey, I said I was doin nuthin' but avin' a drink or two or ten." He spoke this last part expecting to hear the officers order him to walk on.

The light suddenly changed color, narrowing to a beam of intense whiteness. Edwin threw up his hands to shield his eyes as the light shot out across the short distance between them. It struck him, melting his hands, his face, and then disintegrating the rest of his body.

The light went out.

Roman opened his eyes to find himself in an apartment awash with blood and entrails, whose familiar odors had become his choice of smelling salts. His head throbbed its predictable beat, the hangover taking precedent over the effects of last night's change. He'd been dreaming he had a different life. Only now he couldn't quite recall what. Something to do with cheap pulp crime novels.

He sat up, and with it he felt as if the ceiling had suddenly crashed down on him. He squinted against the blur of his hangover and saw Porkchop Bertie's head on a sideboard looking at him with disapproving, unblinking eyes.

"Morning, Porkchop," he said, wondering how he'd feel if Porkchop answered him. These days nothing surprised him.

Porkchop's corpse resembled a shop store mannequin that had seen better days. He was lying on the floor in a state of physical disarray. One of his arms was missing, the other hanging by a thread of pink ligature to the mutilated crenellations of his right shoulder. His torso was a fleshless cavity of splintered rib bones, like the inside of a human musical instrument, intricately mysterious in its exposure.

"You look how I feel," said Roman as he heaved himself from the bed, and shakily took the centre of the room as if daring himself to try any better.

A streak of blood, so crimson it was turning black against the wallpaper, indicated where he'd first hurled Porkchop. A revolver lay near the door to the room. He picked it up, and wondered what they'd done with his own.

There was a wardrobe by the window, a piece of balsa-wood garbage with holes punched in its sides. A pair of grey linen slacks and a black leather jacket hung among several other items of mismatched clothing. They'd have to do. There was no sign of his shoes, which he remembered Pork Chop had removed when he'd decided to stick pins beneath his toe nails. He looked at them, but the wounds were already healing. So were the bruises on his arms and legs. He'd taken quite a beating last night.

Thank God for the moon.

Through an open door leading to the box that was the kitchen a chair lay toppled on the grease-layered linoleum. A pair of shattered handcuffs lay in one corner. The dismembered remains of Porkchop's two bodyguards, including a jawbone strangely positioned on a gas hob on the blood-soaked cooker, told Roman he'd been luckier then usual. The handcuffs indicated they'd been close to putting a bullet in the back of his skull and feeding him to the homeless in one of Porkchop's soup kitchens.

Roman found the communal bathroom on the landing below, a stinking cubbyhole with pages from the Sunday City tabloid supplement pullout calendar for toilet paper. He washed the blood off his face, a routine he'd got used to so quickly he'd hardly had time to consider its psychological implications. He combed his hair with blood-caked fingers. He left the tenement building and stopped a taxi in the middle of the street.

"Hey, Spanno, fancy you driving round these parts," said Roman to the driver. Spanno was barely tall enough to see over the dashboard, let alone the steering wheel, and adjusted the old empty box of Havilland cigars beneath him so he could see better.

"Yeah, guess I must be lost."

"Take me home, Spanno."

"When you say 'home' you mean Duffy's?"

"No, take me to The Gibbous Head?"

Spanno passed Roman a hip flask. "You look like you could do with one."

Roman raised the hip flask to his cracked lips and took a swig. It was as if somebody had poured paraffin down the back of his throat and then tossed in a lit match.

"Jesus, Spanno, if anything was ever illegal, that's the stuff. What is it?"

"Don't ask," said Spanno and floored the taxi as a group of kids in hoods came sauntering round the corner. "Ferals everywhere these days," he muttered, swinging the wheel and round the corner, heading uptown.

Roman took one last look back at the rows of grimy tenements, the abandoned warehouses around which the neighborhood had sprung up like a fungus of architecture resembling the disheveled bums standing round its street corners. He doubted the place had changed much since the turn of the last century.

Spanno left him outside the pub, and a promise to one day reveal the contents of his hip-flask. The pub was already crawling, and Roman had to check the chipped enameled clock behind the bar to make sure it was only a little after eleven.

"No use pretending you're shocked by my clientele's slavish devotion to opening hours. You're here, and from the state of your clothes, I'd say you need a bottle, not just a few pick-me-ups."

Brenda, fifty-five years old, her biceps only lessened in their severity by the orange shading of her skin.

"You'll get skin cancer one day."

"Shut up, and go see Karla," said Brenda, sliding a bottle of whisky with a turkey on the peeling label.

"Where's my usual stuff?"

"Karla says to let you have this on account that you and that policeman friend of yours finished up the last bottles so there weren't any in for the other customers by the time you lot crawled out of here."

"I'll scratch yours, you scratch mine," said Roman, "in a manner of speaking."

"You did a bit of scratching last night."

"News travels fast."

"Apparently body parts travel faster."

Roman uncorked the bottle, picked up a dirty shot glass on the counter, and poured himself a drink.

"Meaning?"

Brenda leaned over the bar and smiled at him, her large unhandsome face reminding him of Porkchop's head on the sideboard.

"Meaning some rookie narc doing a routine sweep of the Dredges found a severed arm lying in the gutter outside of a building known to be frequented by nefarious sorts last night. You were lucky they were pissing too scared to check it out till half an hour ago."

"Luck's a lot like that bottle you just given me, Brenda. Pretty soon it's gonna run out, and when that happens, I'll be right underneath it when it does."

"Go on you bloody fool, Karla's probably watching you on CCTV celebrity channel right as we speaking."

"One thing, Brenda. How come, you said half an hour ago."

"That narc officer buddy of yours was looking for you. I guess he wanted to give you a heads-up or something."

Heads-up. Roman thought of Porkchop again, saw his bloodied head like a decorative knick-knack adorning some grandmother's mantelpiece somewhere.

Karla was in her office surrounded by boxes of supplies for the pub. A single bulb shone down from the peeling surface of the ceiling. A narrow arrow slit like a window with bars across it let in something of the dreariness outside.

"You planning on walking round barefoot all day?" she asked.

Except for the six-inch scar running up the centre of her throat and stopping just short of her bottom lip, she looked like she belonged on a Paris catwalk, and not a gangland mistress. Somehow Roman thought the scar made her look even more attractive.

"Porkchop's got them somewhere," he said, sitting down on a stool that towered over Karla's desk, so that he was looking down on her. She sat back in her chair, curiously officious despite the jeans and short-sleeved blouse. "Don't suppose you've got any flip-flops I can have?"

"Do I look like a flip-flop gal?"

"Maybe when people aren't around to see. I don't know. Are you?"

Karla lifted up one of her legs to show off the steel-capped paratroopers boots she was wearing. "What do you think?"

"I guess I'll have to go all Tarzan on you till I get home."

"You say Porkchop's got them? He's alive?"

"Wrong tense. Porkchop's gone."

"Good. I thought I was going to have to reach inside my desk and pull out something to knock you down off your perch."

"That's why you like having your people up here," said Roman, taking a slug from the bottle. The shot glass was in the pocket of the ill-fitting leather jacket he was wearing.

"Gives me the advantage, not to mention a clean shot through your Adam's apple and up along your trachea."

She didn't know her biology, but Roman thought now wouldn't be a good time to correct her on it.

"Did you want me to kill Bertie?"

"I said follow him. Find out what he was up to."

"I did, and he cottoned on pretty quickly that I was dogging his every step."

"I can still reach in this drawer here," she said, sliding a mani-cured hand over the green ink blotter on her desk. She laughed, as if teasing him, which she wasn't. "It's true my employer wanted Porkchop handled with permanence, but as you know, I'm redirecting company affairs at a more discreet pace."

"Until you're your employer gets out," said Roman.

"Yes, until he gets out," she said, nodding in agreement.

Pop Bang Radiskinksi was a former Olympic Polish weight-lifting champion. He was also the largest exporter of heroin from central Europe into mainland Britain. Shortly after Roman had graduated from police academy, Pop Bang had set up shop. It wasn't long before his exploits for sawing off the legs of his competitors and bench-pressing the torsos onto meat hooks in the freezers of his many restaurants had earned him a reputation equivalent to that of Stanley "Acid Bath" Pilkington from the sixties. He was currently biding his time on a fifteen-year stretch for gun-running from the Ukraine.

With Pop Bang banged up, it was felt by many in The City that the organization might topple faster than a group of tabloid reporters on a sabbatical, but his two sons, Adam and Gregorz, had enthusiastically improved on their father's back catalogue of torture, extortion, and mass murder in quick smart time. In fact, they'd consolidated the family's grip on most of the drug trade in the area that their father had so far failed to do. Mostly. There was still Ton Ton Philippe to contend with.

What Karla didn't know was that Roman had taken the job of Porkchop as a favor to his pal down the precinct. Once a cop, always a cop. But now he wasn't so certain whether he was keeping an eye on Karla and Pop Bang, or the other way round.

"Brenda's got your money," she said, "and something extra because of the unexpected developments."

"That it?" asked Roman. In the bar somebody had managed to get the jukebox working, Gene Pitney's "The Man Who Shot

Liberty Valance" drifting down the corridor and doing its best to sneak into Karla's cluttered office space.

"If you want."

Roman took another gulp from the bottle, corked it, and put it down on the desk.

"Go on."

"How long were you tailing Porkchop?"

"Four days. Eighteen hours out of every twenty-four. Why?"

"How many times did your report back to me in all that time?"

"Three or four."

"Doesn't that strike you as wildly disproportionate to the amount of time spent on the job?"

"He spent most of his time torturing and maiming most of the competition trying to crowbar their way into his business. He was a busy man."

"Apt imagery, Roman."

"Indeed. But you know all this."

"Well, yes and no. Porkchop was always a little exuberant, but until recently I didn't know how much of what I knew or had heard was actually on the authentic side. You know what it's like in a city this size."

"So why have me report on him? Anybody could have done the job."

"Usually that would be true."

"Usually?"

"It's not my money Brenda has for you. In fact, it wasn't even in my interests to put you up for this. Like I said, with my employer languishing inside I've been keeping the business on a more even keel."

Roman suspected Karla's idea of an even keel meant fewer bodies floating to the surface of the Queen Anne river.

"Then whose money was it?"

"An outside party with very little interest in what we do here in the City. Or I should say, little interest in our end of business."

"You mean your end."

"Oh, please, Roman, sweetheart, you've got more blood on your hands for a civilian than most of the imbeciles I keep round here."

"Do these look like civilian clothes to you?" he said, opening his newly acquired leather jacket.

"You look like you're in fancy dress, Roman."

"You should see me when the moon is up."

This time the smile on her face faltered, and he knew she was thinking there was still one more night this month in which he would prowl these City streets in his wolf form.

"I want you to go see this acquaintance of mine. He wants to talk some things over with you."

"Like what?"

"Let him explain."

"Who is he?"

"I'll give you an address."

"And his name."

"Mortley Asperk."

"What kind of name is that?"

"One you won't find in the Yellow Pages."

Karla gave him the address on a piece of paper she ripped off a notepad on her desk. He pocketed it. He never looked at anything until he had his back to a wall and his revolver within easy reach. The one he had on him might not even work. He hadn't bothered checking to see if it was loaded.

"Later, Karla."

At the bar Brenda gave him his money, minus what he owed for the bottle of whisky.

"You revoking my tab?"

"You never had a tab."

Roman stepped outside and squinted against the misery of the city. It was only a ten-minute drive from the Dredges, and it was obvious that Duffy's place, though hardly the Ritz of drinking establishments, was a step up from this neighborhood. He thought he could smell the docks from here, though it might have been the sewers.

Karla had been right about the name. Nothing came up. It made him uneasy. Roman put on a suit that reminded him of his passing-out parade. He looked in the mirror. The suit he'd change out of later. If he timed it right, he'd be in and out of his meeting with Mortley Asperk with several hours before the inevitable monthly transformation.

He took a swig from the bottle of whisky Brenda had charged him for, thought about drinking it all before he headed out, and decided against it. For once he'd go to one of these client meetings sober.

It didn't surprise Roman to find the address was for a new hotel on the other side of town. The area had once rivaled the Dredges, but now the planners and construction companies had come in and started bulldozing people out. The glimmer of steel and glass and expensive cars and sharp-suited bankers gave it the appearance of an alien business district that had landed only yesterday.

Even in his suit, they stopped Roman in the lobby. He asked for Asperk and was shown to an elevator. He passed a bar with young women like starlets sipping gaudy-colored cocktails, while fat men with loose jowls paraded the contents of their wallets through fat fingers dirtier than Pop Bang and Porkchop combined.

"Press for the fifteenth, penthouse," said a man in a suit whose shoulders made battlements of his muscles beneath the straining cloth.

As he rode the elevator, Roman noticed CCTV camera monitoring him from one corner. He thought about smiling for the person at the other end, but he didn't feel in a playful mood, not with the moon ascending tonight.

As expected, two men in suits were waiting for him up top. They looked identical. These guys always did. One of them patted him down.

"This way," said the taller of the two clones, his voice clipped, reminding Roman of the old answer machine recordings.

They walked him down a corridor in silence, one of them in front, the other shadowing him from behind. They reached a door, which opened almost immediately. They ushered him inside, moving him by his elbows.

The door closed behind him, but he didn't look.

The penthouse was like any other, a disgusting shrine to over-indulgence. Its panoramic view of the city was at odds with the gauche, ugly furniture. Sitting on a sofa in a pastel-colored suit which made the man wearing it look like he was on safari, Mortley Asperk stood up to shake Roman's hand. His face was smooth and hairless, as was his head, a round almost spherical-shaped skull.

"Here you are at last, the great-grandfather of all our troubles," said Asperk. His voice was like that of the bodyguard who'd spoken to Roman, flat, modulated.

"Grandfather of what?" said Roman, turning from Asperk, who still had hold of his hand and was quite clearly not going to let go. He turned his head in time to see a glistening hypodermic needle stab into his neck.

Asperk might have been speaking for some time when Roman awoke. He had the perspiring sheen of somebody ranting at a rally, somebody used to addressing hordes of unthinking supporters, his lower lip trembling as he paused to consider one more carefully composed sound bite his speech writer had dreamt up the night before.

Roman didn't try the rope that bound his hands to the back of the chair they'd sat him in. And naturally they'd left his legs loose.

"Take this man, Edwin Sturbridge. A contemporary of yours," said Asperk, his mouth moving. But Roman wasn't really listening because he was staring at the roll of paper dangling from Asperk's hands. It resembled the parchment that men in togas read from as they announced political shenanigans to a senate of overfed politicians baying for more sacrificial blood. Or at least as shown on TV and the movies.

"Who the hell's Edwin Sturbridge?" asked Roman.

Asperk's voice gave that curiously metallic ring again, as if he were modulated by some internal technology, as if his voice were merely a projection of how he thought people should sound.

"A bad, bad man," said Asperk, "Sturbridge was one of the most prolific serial murderers of the early part of the twenty-first century. He disappeared sometime around now, just like your original Jack The Ripper. Interesting similarities, but whereas the Victorian Ripper murdered only prostitutes, Sturbridge murdered anybody who happened to annoy him."

"Was? Past tense? Right. Okay. This the part where you tell me you're from the future?" Roman wasn't kidding. It was one of those days.

Asperk frowned.

"I did have all sorts of future facts and other wonderful tidbits to deliver exposition style, but it seems you're in a bit of hurry to absorb the authenticity of your dilemma."

"You watch a lot of TV where you come from?"

"Twenty-first-century TV was my major," he said, proudly displaying his teeth as if demonstrating the latest in toothpaste whitener. "I'm also one of the few people trained to speak twenty-first-century English. Chinese and Indian, too."

"I thought you might be outrageously homosexual."

"Where I come from there's no outrage in sexuality at all. That stopped short of the twenty-fourth century with UNISEX."

"I thought unisex was clothing for all," Roman almost sang. "Anyway, that's not what I meant."

"I'm not sure if your antiquarian humor is going to hit all the marks."

"You sound kinda funny," said Roman, "and I'm not talking about all these lines of dialogue nobody outside of a movie would bother using."

The moon wasn't yet visible from the window, a bank of cloud sullying the thousands of lights. splintering the City into columns and blocks. Roman was playing for time, just like every good detective bound to a chair should, but with the two bodyguards standing out of sight, he knew he'd have to wait till the moon was riding high above the opulent architecture of the skyscrapers before he could do anything about it.

A twinge in his left shoulder said he had about forty minutes before he changed.

"Listen, Aspert."

"Asperk," he corrected.

"Aspert, Asperk, Asshole, whatever. You mind explaining why you had me wasting my time following Porkchop Bertie?"

"I don't know any Porkchop Bertie," he said. He glanced over at the bodyguards, who'd stepped into Roman's eyesight, just to his left, near the window. "Was he on the list? Check histories for me." Asperk flapped the roll of parchment, then flung it behind him. "I don't need that anymore. That was purely for show."

"You paid Karla Zielinska, who coincidentally works for Pop Bang, to dog Porkchop and his crew."

"Interesting names," said Asperk.

"You can talk."

"I don't know any Porkchop. I do know of a Mr. Kaminski. We have him down on the list somewhere." Asperk nudged the scroll of paper with his foot. "Pop Bang, as you say. And I do know Miss Karla, this is true. In fact, I asked her to send you here."

"Why didn't you just pick up the phone and ring yourself?"

"I find introductions through other people, especially those you trust, makes the odds slightly more in one's favor."

"I did a job for her. That doesn't mean I trust her. There's a big difference between a woman paying your bills and the one you wake up to. Though sometimes I get the two mixed up."

Asperk laughed, but it was brittle, unconvincing.

"How'd you get her to do want you want? She's a tough lady."

"It was easy when I showed her this," Asperk said, motioning to the bodyguards.

"What is it?" asked Roman.

The bodyguards carried a three-foot-long cylindrical tube across the room, placing it on the sofa next to where Asperk was standing. At one end of the tube a blue light flared, its source seemingly invisible since the tube appeared hollow. At the other end what looked like a trigger curled upwards.

"I could explain its complexities to you, but I doubt your twenty-first-century brain would be able to fathom what I was telling you. Let's just say that it's a weapon which simply erases dangerous anomalies and abnormalities from whatever period we need to clean up."

"Right. This time travel thing of yours. What century did you say you were from?"

"I didn't, but it's toward the beginning of the next millennium."

"Nice."

"Yes, it is. Except for the war."

"Some things never change, huh." Roman's left shoulder twitched, unseen by Asperk and hopefully his men. A fiery line of pain shot down the centre of his spine, like a hammer hitting keys of bone.

"To be truthful, Mr. Dalton, they've changed...considerably. All—except, that is, the outbreak of lycanthropy. This nuisance of a war. Like every hereditary disease, we need to stop it before it spreads any further."

Roman laughed, despite the pain.

He glanced out the window. The moon was above the nearest skyscraper. Fat and swollen and ready to sing its wonderful lullaby of pain.

"What's all this got to do with this fella Sturbridge, Karla, Porkchop, and some war that hasn't yet happened?"

"Sturbridge was merely a point of reference for me to clarify my point. And this weapon," he said, and sat down on the sofa. He looked at Roman and smiled, and moved it aside so he had more room.

"You see, I'm a representative of a political party whose incumbent administration are trying to explain to the people of our time that the war with lycanthrope terrorists is down to our political opponents. We know it is. They know it is. But the people don't know it is. We decided to come back and do either of two things to rectify the situation."

"I thought you guys weren't allowed to tamper with time."

"You're speaking about the tenets of time traveling as eloquently displayed in any number of Hollywood movies?"

"I think," said Roman. He felt his carotid artery pumping faster than usual. He should have changed by now.

"I work in Calculations, Mr. Roman—probably, apart from our colleagues in Actual Projections, the most important department involved. It's our responsibility to see if or what will change if we interfere, or, in the case of Mr. Sturbridge, how future timelines up to our own period will be affected. Sometimes there are changes, but most of these are innocuous alterations that nobody will miss."

"You mean you wipe people out here, and to hell with the consequences."

"The consequences if we don't far outweigh those that we do."

"Isn't that a bit like being judge and jury?"

"You forgot executioner."

"It's not funny."

"I didn't say it was."

"So this Sturbridge was removed from the timeline?"

"Exactly. We calculated that those who were rendered nonexistent because of his erasure made no difference to our present."

"If you're so concerned about saving people, why didn't you go back before he started killing people?"

"We are only interested in saving people from our own period, Mr. Dalton. And some of those people he killed had a direct influence on our future. Alteration is one thing, but too much of it would play havoc with our present."

"You ever watch a Hollywood movie on time travel?"

"Of course. I'm also a historian."

"Then you'd know most of them have plot holes so glaring it would be impossible to do what you claim."

"I wouldn't expect you to understand. Let's put it this way — we know what we're doing."

"I don't believe you."

"After everything we've shown you."

"You haven't shown me anything. Just that tin-pipe contraption there."

"You ever dream you lived another life? That you were never a policeman, weren't a lycanthrope?"

Roman remembered the half-dreamt remnants of the dream he'd had in Porkchop's flat. It didn't prove a thing.

"Okay, if you fucked up my original timeline, why? That'd mean you made me the source of your future so-called werewolf terrorists."

"That's the point."

"What's the point?"

"Work it out, Mr. Dalton. It's time we got you prepared for your trip."

"Right, the future," said Roman. "Just one thing before we go."

"Yes?"

"Zielinska gave me something to stop the transformation, right?"

Asperk grinned, all pretension gone now.

"She said you liked a drink."

"Something from the future, I suppose?"

"An inhibitor. Doesn't last for too long, which is why we need to hurry."

"Thought so," said Roman. "That cheap whisky Brenda gave me."

The moon looked larger above the nearest building, what had once been a slum tenement but had been recently converted into loft apartments.

"Usually I drink two or three bottles a day, easy," said Roman, his biceps flexing involuntarily. "But today I decided to give it a rest after last night's escapades, and 'cause I was expected here."

Asperk reached for the weapon on the sofa, almost screaming.

It was too late.

By the time he got his finger 'round the trigger, Roman had changed, swatting aside one of the security guards through the penthouse window, bitten through the throat of the second bodyguard, and clamped his great lupine jaws over Asperk's entire right arm.

The weapon dropped to the floor, Asperk's hand still attached.

Roman waited two days before he revisited Karla. He found her in an apartment not far from where he'd eaten Asperk. The irony wasn't wasted on him.

"Pop Bang never wanted Porkchop dead, did he?"

There was no full moon, so Roman pointed the revolver against Karla's temple, his trigger finger slick with anticipation.

"You've been speaking to his sons." She didn't even look at him, just uncrossed her legs, lifted her cigarette to her mouth, and looked at the mirror across her fancy apartment. "The moon ain't up, honey, what you going to do, tickle me to death with that thing?"

"I'm not one for drawn-out denouements," said Roman and pulled the trigger.

One month later he had that dream again. The one with him at a typewriter, the one where he was a crime writer of cheap pulps. He woke up and reached for a bottle and thought the idea was absurd.

———

Frank Duffy is the author of the collection *The Signal Block and Other Stories* and the novelette *Mountains of Smoke*. He lives in Warsaw with his wife and two dogs. His blog is "The Signal Block."

GETTING HIGH ON DAISY

Richard Godwin

ROMAN DALTON AWOKE IN AN EMPTY FLAT beneath a silver moon and picked a sliver of metal from his teeth. He stumbled into the peeling bathroom and stared at his ashen face beneath the flickering light, a million miles from sanity. Images raced through his mind like isolated scenes in a film. Men standing over him with baseball bats, a woman's face with eyelashes that looked unnaturally long, a shallow grave, metal bars against his mouth. He could taste the cold hard steel.

He spat blood into the sink and brushed his teeth with the dirty brush that lay at its edge, squeezing out the last of the hardened toothpaste. Then he walked out into the deserted streets, relying on a memory that seemed someone else's to steer him towards his destination. He didn't know the flat nor what dark transit had escorted him there. He had no recollection of the preceding days. All he knew was that with each change the moon his master invoked, more of him was stolen and the record of memory was lost. He felt The City around him like a caul. It held the past in its clenched fist like the promise of identity, like a map of history, and Roman headed towards its dark and silent heart, his footsteps clacking on the paving stones.

Roman had first had the flashes as a child. Waking screaming in the night, he'd pierced his father's eardrums and watched him stagger with bleeding lobes into the darkened hallway.

And now as Roman Dalton found his office, he was faced with the picture of a woman he knew but could not remember on his desk.

Hazel eyes set in an alabaster face stared at him out of a sepia background, and he felt the scratching of an episode at the cuff of his coat. He looked at the calendar. Days had passed, mail was stacked up at the door. What had stolen time like this? He must have lain in that flat for nights.

He knew that the dislocation of man from beast was a place of nothing, a descent where he knew nothing, felt empty, barren of identity. The beast was alive, the man he was had been bled dry by the violence of the inner rage. The howling was life. This stumbling back to the hairless body was like being shaved of self and starved of vitality. He knew another cycle was coming on.

He sat and drank two fingers of Glennfiddich and felt the warmth work its way into his empty bell and he stared at a spot on the ceiling, summoning the knowledge he knew from feral depths that were tideless in the information they held. It was always a churning noise he heard first, as if someone held a container of water and was shaking it in his ear. This gave way to a sudden silence that was deafening, and then the images started, like a parade of characters he did not know played out on an unstoppable film. They rarely spoke, but when they did he listened. Ever since the first childhood episode, it was the same when it came on. It was like being planted in someone else's story.

He remembered knowing who the school thief was and nailing him to some railings while his other hand punched him until he was caked in blood. It was always his other hand, or the hand of the other, as he thought of it back then, a straggly teenager built of muscle and bone with a wild look in his eyes. He could smell which girls were menstruating as clearly as he smelled the sizzling meat at the local Wimpy.

Roman headed out into the bleak streets, dodging the early crack addicts who bared gold teeth at him and looked away as he turned his black animal eyes on them and kicked open the door of MacDonalds.

The meat was always overcooked, and he hungered for blood, the deep dark blood that spelled its own ruination and division from the affairs of men. He remembered the first time he ate raw steak, cooking for his father and peeling away a strip and popping it in his mouth and feeling whole again, not this dismembered beast howling for identity.

He looked at the early diners, their grey faces a pattern of weakness, and he knew he was being called to solve another case.

A narrative written by a pen with barely drying ink was wending its way through his mind. He knew he had to find Daisy, and he had no idea who she was.

He returned to his office and stared at the photograph and knew. He had to enter her world to find the way back. The blackouts were becoming more frequent, the erasing of his days the norm. He sweated for drink and bit his cheek to ward off the craving, looking at the clock on the wall and thinking, It's only eight it's only eight. What space may my troubled heart find to rest while it is hunted by this beast?

He would find her and end this drama. He would know what had happened.

She was in London. He would journey from The City.

He wound through the streets, past Plato Road, and made his way to Stockport tube station, seeing the wilting flowers set there for the Brazilian boy, smelling his blood and the lies of the police on the piss-stained hopeless London paving blocks, and their memories of midnight hatred and despair.

In the station a busker plays Steely Dan's "Haitian Divorce," and it comes to him.

He is there. It has the immediacy of a distinct physical experience.

In his mind's eye beneath the rattle of the train he can see her, he can smell her.

She has a thing for duck. She eats it with her fingers, licking them one by one. She likes to feel it slide down her throat.

"So, Harry, you're looking a little nervous," she says.

A small dimly lit cafe crackles into view. The hiss of eggs on a greasy pan.

She can smell Harry's wealth. She has it, too. She is one, she is wolf. She's an addict, she chose to be to ward off the alterations. She's using more and more, needing more and more to keep them at bay. Sometimes at night she wakes with a bleeding mouth and cuts herself, all the tricks, Roman knows, in the end fail to work. She knows sex like a chameleon adventuress trapped in a dream. She remembers watching the rich folk eat duck as a kid and how when she started making money she bought it all the time.

She's wearing a long red satin dress, and she places one Sergio Rossi stiletto on the chair between his legs, the heel touching his cock.

It is over a hundred degrees outside. Harry dabs his brow. He looks around the empty restaurant.

"Oh, baby," Daisy says, "want mamma to cool your fever down?"

Harry has a tanned face with a birthmark that stretches from his hairline and fades into pale strawberry at his eyebrows. He often wears a hat to hide it. He hates it and resents people with good complexions.

"I want you to dominate me," Harry says.

He's lying, Roman thinks, watching the film in his mind, unaware of his surroundings.

Harry looks at Daisy, following the flow of thick black hair that cascades across her shoulders, taking in her hazel eyes set provocatively in a face full of sexual knowing.

"I know you do it well, I hear you're the best," he says.

"I know my whips, baby, if it's bondage you want."

"That's why I called you."

"Is it a house call?"

"It is."

"My fees are half up front."

Harry reaches into his pocket and passes her a wad of notes, which she counts with fingers covered in duck grease. The fatty smell mingles with the odour of used notes.

In the vision Roman can smell her cunt.

She is on heat, a rare bitch with bridled tendencies, swaddled in the ways she's used to survive alone like him in the world of men. He can see her harnessed, the chain around her throat, the wild eyes of sexual refusal beneath the masquerade of yielding.

"Thank you for the duck," she says. "You obviously know about me. What about you, Harry? What are you after?" Her eyes drift to his birthmark. "I specialise in all forms of dominance.

You want a little burning?"

"I tie myself up," Harry says.

"Oh, do you?"

"I want you to come in and find me like that."

"Okay, honey."

The train stops. Roman looks ahead of him, the vision like a headache he cannot shed until it's over. There are no pills for this agony, nothing can alleviate this dissection of the soul.

It is like erupting from a womb and yet the womb is yours. The birthrights of time and the evolution of the species cast away in the fractured flesh.

Two youths in tattered jeans sit staring at him.

He shuts his eyes and lets the film continue, the chugging train the rhythm to which he clings as the world about him fades.

It is a blue twilight as her shadow falls across the lawn.

Harry is drinking whisky and watching from the window as she walks up the drive to the back door and opens it. He goes to get ready. Daisy moves slowly; she has an air of control in her movements. She enters by the kitchen as arranged and climbs the stairs, shedding her coat at the top. She stands in leather. She is wearing Giuseppe Zanotti stilettos, and she pulls a whip from her bag.

She enters the first room and finds him slumped in a chair, his head hanging forward, the light dimmed. She looks down at his cock, which lies across his thigh with a purple vein running along it.

She lights a cigarette and blows smoke on it.

"Feeling a little groggy, Harry?" she says.

She starts to rub his cock, lifting a leg to expose her waxed cunt beneath the leather skirt.

He groans.

She presses the heel of her stiletto against his cock.

"Are you going to do what I say?" she says. "You haven't tied these ropes well, have you, let mamma do it, and then you can do some dirty things for me, you will be my dirty boy."

In sex she keeps the howling at bay, Roman thinks, no one knows how to enter her.

As she bends to fasten the ties on his hands, she notices his forehead seems free of the birthmark. She wonders if it is a trick of the light.

Suddenly he lifts his hands up and wraps them around her neck.

He pulls her forward and starts to choke her.

Daisy kicks out and hits him in the head with her heel. It sticks in his cheek, and it pulls away a piece of flesh as she puts her leg down and reaches in her bag. He is getting out of the chair as she turns and hits him with the taser. She hits him twice in the chest and he falls. She stands over him.

Harry watches all of this from the door.

Daisy leans and checks for a pulse.

"Daisy, meet my twin brother," Harry says, coming into the room. "He had a weak heart."

"You don't do this to me."

"That's why he was given more money by the family. They didn't approve of me. They didn't like my birthmark. Of course I wasn't going to let them get away with that. Your reputation with a taser precedes you. You see, my background is in research. I'm a head hunter. You're good. Just what I want."

He walks over and touches her. He runs his hand across her cunt as she pulls away and starts to dress.

He smells his hand and narrows his eyes, noticing the strange feral odour.

He can see her hands are shaking.

She reaches into her bag and drops a pill.

"I'm getting out of here," she says.

"That would be rash, wouldn't it, Daisy? It's all on CCTV."

He points to the camera.

Daisy looks at him, registers he is standing outside the range.

"You know all about dominance and the roles people play. Someone has to submit. My brother hated being tied up," he says. "I did it to him once when we were kids and he went crazy."

"What do you want?" she asks.

"You, Daisy. I just bought you, you're going to be my whore."

The train stops. Roman doesn't open his eyes despite the fact that he can sense the two youths are standing over him.

There is more, he thinks, there is more. I have to find her.

Harry sits in a restaurant with Ton Ton Philippe.

He picks his teeth with a toothpick, looking at the strand of grey meat hung there.

"It's a long time since Haiti," Harry says.

Ton Ton nods.

"So what do you want me to do with her?" he says.

"Use the puffer fish."

"You want this whore zombiefied?"

"I do."

"What are you, a fucking necrophiliac?"

Harry peels open an envelope and hands him the cash.

"I like to take a spirited whore and tame her, tether her, and make her my fuck thing."

"My drugs will slow down anything."

Ton Ton flicks the edge of the notes, relishing their mint crispness in the air. He lays two black eyes on Harry.

"She needs to be reduced to nothing more than the murmur of a heartbeat, a tremor in her chest like a lightly fluttering bird's wing." Harry shrugs.

"Sure."

"When we take her out of the earth you will fuck your whore, it will be an experience like no other, she will be like butter."

"Now you're talking," Harry says, and pops a potato in his mouth.

As Roman opens his eyes, he hears the swish of the blade in the air and moves forward, head-butting the wielder in the stomach. He takes and lifts the other by the throat and hurls him against the window.

The knife wielder is lying on the floor looking up as Roman kicks him in the face and launches his head across the tube like a football.

He will not move again, he thinks, as he heads out into Kilburn tube station, thinking, *How did I come this far?*

"Bring me my Latvian whores that I may scald their soft skins," Harry said.

He was reclining on a couch. A woman dressed in a leather thong was popping grapes in his mouth. He looked like a congenitally insane Roman emperor. He was positioned so that the side of his face that bore the birthmark was not visible.

He waved a hand in a histrionic gesture.

"I want them brought naked one by one."

The grape bearer bowed and left the room, which was cavernous in its size. Marble covered the floors and Dutch tiles the walls. At the centre of the room was a fountain. The water spouted from a hydra's head, and its gurgling was faintly soporific.

A parade of naked women entered the room.

Harry looked at each and dismissed them with a click of his fingers until one came in and he stood to examine her.

She was darker than the rest and had something of the animal about her. She held his stare with defiant eyes, and Harry became aroused.

He approached her and touched her, lifting her breasts in

both hands before feeling her cunt.

As he did she struck him sharply across the face.

At first he was dumbfounded, having no immediate response for this challenge.

Then he motioned to her to sit down.

She did in a chair opposite his couch. He crossed the room to a fire which burned at the opposite end and fetched a glowing poker from its flames. Then, approaching her from behind, he branded the side of her face, holding her back in the chair.

She tried to fight but he began to beat her, hitting her squarely with a large ring that held a ruby.

He opened up her eye and knocked her to the floor, where he kept hitting her until she was unconscious.

Then he raised his toga and climbed on top of her.

Harry Nero had made his money from skips. He'd progressed to a haulage business and used his millions to indulge his taste for rough sex. Like any addict he soon needed more extreme kicks to fill the raging void at the centre of his corrupted heart. He got involved in the sex slave scene and bought a large mansion in London where he housed his harem, to which he retired at night for the indulgences that made him feel alive. For Harry had always felt dead inside. Ever since he was a small boy he had suffered from nightmares that he would be eaten alive by a wolf.

He hated his twin brother for his clear complexion. He thought he had stolen his identity.

Harry had a penchant for sexual torture from a young age. As a small boy he'd put a hot iron against his sister's face and left a permanent strawberry stain there that ran deep into her hairline. He wanted everyone to know what it felt like to carry a red stain on their flesh.

After he burned his sister he called her Berry and used to watch her shower through a hole he drilled in the bathroom wall.

He'd stand in the cupboard next to it as a teenager and watch her, knowing the burn turned him on more than her nudity.

She never recovered and suffered from depression, committing suicide in her late teens. Harry found her body and his father found him standing over her corpse with an erection and pulling up her nighty. He broke Harry's nose and threw him out of the house. Harry's mother died a few months later and he never saw his father again, never spoke of him.

He kept in touch with his twin. He got a job in the stock exchange, became a good trader, and made enough to start his own business after a few years and never looked back.

His proclivity for extreme sex increased in direct commensurate relation to his wealth.

He met Ton Ton on a trip to Haiti. He'd gone there because of his fascination with voodoo.

He wanted to see the religion in action. He wanted to fuck a horse in trance. Ton Ton had served him local whores, and he'd learned to cut them with religious ritual.

He'd given Ton Ton a sizeable sum of money to find him women who had a feral allure, since tethering and taming were the biggest turn-ons to him.

"Taming a compliant victim means nothing to me," he said. "I want them wild and hurt."

The night he left Haiti the Ton Ton Macoutes were out in force. Papa Doc was in his ascendancy and everyone feared Baron Samedi. Harry loved the sweet smell of graveyards at midnight. He stared through the sunglasses of the Ton Ton Macoutes, which they wore even at night, and saw his own dead eyes there beneath them, as if they were merely a mirror to his soul.

Ton Ton found Daisy on one of his trips to The City. He would regularly checks the ads for hookers, looking for the unusual ones who provided the kind of service that indicated they were to Harry's taste. He arranged for them to meet.

After Daisy killed Harry's twin, he shot her full of elephant tranquillizer. She clawed him and he punched her before raping her on the floor as she lay comatose. He and Ton Ton took her out of The City and to London. They put her in one of the cells he had in his harem. Harry spent one whole night fucking her repeatedly, scoring a deep cut on her buttock with a razor from which blood poured onto his white silk sheets.

Daisy awoke in a locked room and hammered on the door until her fists were bleeding.

She saw the wound and felt bruised inside, and she searched the room for weapons, finding none.

She was locked in for days with no nourishment or water, and when they did enter the room with food she was too weak to stand.

When they left she ate and staggered to the curtains. She drew them and stared at the sky, willing the moon to grow in fullness that it might give her the power to fight them and escape.

She dreamed of wolves and howled for a mate.

She fought Harry each time he came in to cut and fuck her, and held fragments of his skin beneath her sharp nails. He and Ton Ton tied her down and Harry pared her nails back so that she barely had any, removing one entirely with pliers so her fingers were raw. He put a lit match to the wound and said, "That'll teach you to scratch me, bitch."

Daisy stared at him with canine eyes.

Harry smashed her in the mouth, opening up her lip.

One night as a full moon rose in the sky they came in and drugged her.

"We're going to bury you in the ground, then I'm going to bugger you," Harry said.

Daisy was drifting from consciousness just as her alteration kicked in.

And Harry and Ton Ton headed out into a wild and moonlit night.

Roman knows her, he knows them all, has studied them through the red eyes of the moon scudding overhead as his life tilts backwards on a razor.

He heads towards the Wolf and Bone, the pub a blur in his vision, as he feels the blood racing in his veins. He knows the howling is only moments away as darkness begins to settle. To him it feels like moths falling on his skin.

Micky is in the back, polishing glasses. He gives him a half glance and opens the door to the stockroom.

He looks at Micky, the stubble on his face, he is unchanged since childhood, he bears only the usual aging of man, not this inner canine violence to the soul and its recurrent tides. He envies him for a moment, wonders what such continuity must feel like, and remembers he is what this savagery has made him.

"Roman, what's up?" Micky says.

"I need your help."

"Of course."

"I need to find her."

Micky stares at the picture of Daisy, thinking she has the face of a whore, as Roman reads him, feeling fur about his ankles rising like some tide.

"Yeah, she used to work the streets before she went private, caters to some rich dicks now who like a little whipping. Why you looking for her?"

"A job."

"Funny job to save a whore."

Roman looks at him. It is a look Micky knows well from

when they grew up. He remembers things he can't explain.

He hands him a piece of paper with an address written on it, and Roman drinks a shot of whisky at the bar before heading there in a black cab.

All the way the taxi driver prattles on as the memories return, accompanying the nocturnal change as accomplices in his denaturing.

The world is fading, its seams exposed. It is splitting like a coat losing its stuffing, the blur of the lost days that led to the flat gaining focus.

The flashes are becoming more intense now, bringing shooting pains in the side of his head. He remembers.

He is looking for Daisy. He once knew her flesh.

He knows she is in danger, and two men step out of the shadows with bats.

Ton Ton has sent them. Roman is on a job, and he has sent them after him. They track him down to a moonlit car lot. They corner him as the silver light steams across the waxed immaculate bodies of Fords. They wear Halloween masks baring teeth, and they hit him as he turns. Then they flee into the night as Roman snaps at the railings.

Ton Ton has killed Hooded Cane, the man who helped Roman escape from Haiti. All those years ago, zombified by Ton Ton on a desolate beech. Cane rescued him. Ton Ton's toxin was too weak against the violence of the change Roman was going through. Roman tore a chunk out of Ton Ton's leg. The scar is still there; it itches on a full moon.

Hooded Cane knew what Roman is, knew Lupus. He put him on a boat. Roman locked himself in his cabin, thirsty with a rabidity that made his teeth ache. Aching all the way until he made The City again.

He remembers finding Cane's body.

He is standing in the flat, the address he has for him, wondering where he has gone.

He has hired Roman to find Daisy. Cane is trying to crack a gang of sex slaves. Ton Ton is at the top, an expert in the sale of female flesh.

Roman is standing in the flat and sees a shape on the floor. He approaches. It is Cane. His chest is black. Ton Ton has removed his heart.

Roman goes through to the peeling bathroom and sees his face in the mirror. He is changing. It is a peak alteration.

He heads out into the night, passing through an alley that runs alongside the car lot as Ton Ton's men find him.

They hit him and Roman feels blood in his hands.

A full moon rides a violent sky and he is howling.

He tears at their flesh, leaving a gaping wound, and they flee.

He sees them through railings. He has his teeth set against them and he bites the metal and he smells their fear as they run. He will pursue them.

He wants meat, he wants raw bleeding meat, something to sink his fangs into. He can hear bones breaking, his hands are tearing bones apart as he ducks into an alley and sits, legs tucked beneath him howling, thinking these are the cries of pain, there is no mercy in pain.

He is back there. There is no time in the howling, it is zero zone.

He can smell her, he can smell Daisy's sex as she climbs into bed with him. All those years ago, the two of them like rabid dogs clutching at what they gave. He is further on than her, the changes taking away the record of his actions, leaving him stranded with only the howling. He knew then she would trade in what she had. He feels it again, the high of entering her like a shot of heroin in his veins and her yielding. She is smack, she is opium, her lips and cunt intoxicate him. She profits from the exotic thrill her body carries, the danger of fucking the wild and available woman of night.

He once removed his finger from her cunt after she'd come and run it around his gums. He had the anaesthetic numbing sensation that cocaine gives to the gum, only stronger.

He used to crave her. Her skin was like some narcotic that made his entire being alive with arousal, she smelled of feral flowers, the nocturnal blossoms of she wolf fecundity. She opened herself to him and he entered her world and together they feasted on the high of their aloneness, sharing the pain of their exile from the world of man.

He needed more and more of her and they tore at each other with claws and the craving of addiction. He used to wake with deep long furrows in his back, pits of congealed blood matted against the sheets, which stuck to him as he rose. She would pull him inside her and howl, her red eyes set against his as she laid her mouth on his, their fangs clashing.

Only the recurrent changes took the memory of her away.

It lay like an unearthly dream buried at the bottom of his mind.

He is gaining on them. Roman finds the woods. He can smell the men's blood from the road. There is the rank odour of sexual arousal in the air. There are trees all around him. He can smell earth now.

As he approaches, he hears the beating of their pulses.

They are standing over the grave, and he can smell Daisy there beneath the dampened earth.

It is beginning to rain, a light pitter-patter.

He gets high, floats, above them all, knowing. His brain is

shot through with a drug more powerful than morphine, and the accompanying hunger for her sets in.

Daisy is asleep, her pulse slowed by the toxin, and Harry is standing with an erection, ready to pounce, wanting to own her as a small toy he can fuck and abandon.

Ton Ton lights a cigarette, the end glowing like a firefly in the black air.

"She will rise shortly, we'll dig her up," Ton Ton says. "Are you ready to rape your zombie bride? She'll never see The City again."

"I want to lance the whore's flesh," Harry says. "She'll yield nicely now; she's shackled to me."

Roman edges to within inches of them.

The word has gone red. His teeth are bared.

Ton Ton turns, in slow motion now, and reaches into his pocket as Roman launches at him, sinking his fangs into his throat, knocking the gun from his hand. He is shaking his head in his jaws and eating his face, a quarter gone now as bone juts through the thin wrapping of his skin. He tears out his throat and raises his head as blood pumps up from Ton Ton's neck.

Harry is running through the woods. He is panting hard as he heads towards his car and Daisy rises from the grave like a nightmare bride.

Roman gains ground on Harry, finds him at the door, and bites into his face, ripping out an eye. He can hear his bones crunching. He holds him to the earth and tears out his heart.

The taste of the meat increases his hunger. He raises his head and howls at the moon that rides the sky.

He can smell her.

She is there in the trees, awakening from their attempt to steal her.

He goes to her and she reaches out a hand, her nails lengthening from her fingers.

Soon they are in the wild earth lost in the enterprise of their becoming, her heat upon him.

He enters her again, seeing the red eyes of her face.

They howl beneath the swollen moon.

Richard Godwin is the author of the bestselling crime novel *Apostle Rising* and is a widely published crime and horror writer. His second novel, *Mr. Glamour*, is out now and is available online at Amazon and at all good retailers. It is about a glamorous world with a predator in its midst and is already attracting great reviews. His "Chin Wags at the Slaughterhouse" are interviews he has conducted with writers and can be found at his blog on his website at richardgodwin.net, where you can also find a full list of his works. He lectured in English and American literature at London University before becoming a professional writer.

SILVER TEARS

John Donald Carlucci

"Jesus, I think I stepped on an ear," I said after nearly slipping and falling as I entered the taped-off crime scene. "Don't you guys check out the area first anymore?"

"Sorry," said one of the CSI techs as he sheepishly rushed over to photograph and collect the piece of errant flesh.

I can't really blame him, as the murder scene was bloody awful, and that's saying a lot coming from an ex-police detective and current werewolf.

I caught my old partner's eye and waved him over.

"Roman, what are you doing here?" Detective Ivan Walker asked as he grabbed my shoulder tightly. His scarred face was incapable of conveying any subtle emotions properly, but fear is something I can smell easily. Lowering his voice, Walker leaned in close. "This woman was torn to pieces, and it looks like an animal did it."

"It wasn't me," I said. "You know this isn't my thing."

"Where were you, then?"

"Drunk and sleeping with the green fairy." The little bitch was behind my eyes hitting everything real hard with her little fairy sledgehammer.

"You weren't out prowling?" Walker asked suspiciously.

"Full moon isn't for two days."

"Son-of-a-bitch, you're right," Walker said as he let go of my shoulder and exhaled deeply."

"I didn't know you cared so much."

"Bugger off."

"There it is," I said, smiling. Walker was never a morning person; I guess tremendous pain can alter a person's outlook. Oh, yeah, becoming a snarly man-beast once a month can, too.

"Why are you here, then, Roman?"

People misunderstand what a werewolf really is. Of course, this is quite understandable, as most people only have fiction, legends, and movies to go by. I have first-hand knowledge.

I'm a wolf every day of my life. It's only during the full moon that the creature can truly express itself. But there are times when I experience a greater sense of smell, taste, sight, and hearing. I can run a bit faster than a normal bloke, lift more than I could in the past, and I'm always goddamned horny. I can't believe how many times I've been embarrassed by a woody when some chick has passed me on the street and she has just finished her period. I guess that's why I drink so much.

I was hired by this fellow to find his runaway daughter last week and I nicked a pair of her panties while searching her room. Yeah, pretty pervy. However, I needed her scent to track her down. Unfortunately, scent-tracking while in human form is nowhere near the same as when I'm a wolf.

"I'm working a runaway case, and it looks like I found her."

"God, there isn't any way the parents will recognize her from that mess."

"They don't have to. I know it's her."

"The old sniffer, then?" Walker asked.

"Yes, the sniffer." I gave my ex-partner the hairiest eyeball I could. "Someday, we need to have a talk about why you know so much."

"Maybe someday."

On a far hill overlooking the horrific crime scene, a sweaty and unpleasant man lifts his camera, with a terrifically large tele-photo lens, to his eye and clicks several images of the two men talking.

"My, my, who have we here?"

Walker allowed me to enter the crime scene, and I found myself a bit queasy seeing the nightmare that was done to this girl. Funny thing, coming from someone who had done worse to the scum of this city just last month.

The coroner, Doctor Taylor, was inspecting what was left of the girl's womb.

"Roman, quite a surprise seeing you here," he said with genuine warmth. "You've been missed."

"Thanks, Doc, you're going to make me tear up in a manly way."

"If you girls are done braiding each other's hair," Walker said as he crouched down at Taylor's side. "Roman was working this case before she died."

"A shame."

"So, you think an animal did this?" I asked as I stared at the mess of human puzzle pieces. Something was wrong, but I couldn't put my finger on it.

"The maul marks are huge. It almost appears to be a bear or lion attack."

"Not a wolf?" Walker asks.

"No, the claw marks are huge. I don't know of a wolf large enough to have a paw this size." Taylor held his hand over a distinctive and defined tear in the girl's flesh. "This one is bigger than my hand."

That's when I realized what was bugging me.

"I think you're wrong, Doc," I said crouching down and taking a pencil from my pocket. Using the eraser end, I lifted a small flap of skin where the claw marks for this wound started. "Each of the tears of this claw wound are the same depth. Claws or hands don't work this way."

"What's he saying?" Walker asked.

"I see what you're getting at, Roman." Taylor smiled as he reexamined the wound. "You should have been a coroner, detective."

"Doc!" Walker said with growing frustration.

"When a hand or claw digs into anything, you expect to find different depth paths for each digit because the hand is a flexible appendage. These wounds show consistent depth patterns you would only find if a tool was used."

"Like a fake claw?" Walker said as he stared at the wound.

"A taxidermy bear claw would do it," I said, tossing my bloodied pencil away.

"So, we have a killer out there who fancies himself a beast," Taylor said as Walker and I locked eyes.

"He's not the first."

"Funny, Walker," I said with enough ice to chill a gallon of vodka—which is exactly what I went looking for as I left that horrid little spot.

Rolling on his back and staring at the sky, the horrid man laughed. Watching this newcomer sniff the air the way he had convinced him that he had found one of the beasts. Gathering his things and rushing for his car, he knew he had a lot of research to do and only a few days to do it in.

I put off calling the father because two bottles of Dark Valentine didn't give me the slightest bit of liquid courage. I ended up vomiting copious amounts of liquor and an unsatisfying pint of pork fried rice with three spring rolls on the sidewalk. Duffy made sure I got home alive, and that's the last I remembered before the hands of an alcoholic amnesia claimed me.

The horrid man stared at his photocopy-covered walls and was pleased. Everything was here, from Roman's police record, his accident, leave of absence, and moon charts comparing his retirement from the force and his accident. Sweat poured down his face and soaked his pale and unpleasant body. The pungent aroma of body odor, excitement, and blood filled the air in the large warehouse room. Soon he wouldn't need fake limbs and synthetic claws to kill his prey.

He'd be a beast in body as well as soul.

With Roman's address and a large rifle case in hand, he knew he had one more bit of evidence to gather to be certain.

I awoke with my hair glued to my sweat-soaked pillow by copious amounts of dried vomit. Last night had been bad and one of the worst I've had in a long time. Peeling myself free, I settled in for a nice long shower as I tried to wash away the waste and despair coating my body in equal measure.

Being refreshed was something I'd long since given up on, and clean was the best I could settle for. I stood under the spray until the hot ran out and cold chilled me to the bone.

I left the apartment dressed in my uniform of black jeans, Doc Martins, black T-shirt, and black trench coat. Duffy waited in the front seat of his car with his rear door ajar. I have to ask him how he always knows when I'm leaving my apartment.

I didn't hear a thing before the freight train slammed into my chest, spraying blood about like a punctured water balloon. I managed to stay on my feet as I spun in a full 180-degree circle, thanks to the impact. It felt like a mini-sun had exploded in my chest, and I was ready to combust in flames. I grabbed the cab door and threw myself into the back seat.

"Jesus Christ!" Duffy yelled as he half-lunged over the front seat to help me.

"Doctor Frankenstein," was all that I could croak out before my old friend oblivion crashed in on me once again.

The horrid man could barely contain the joy that washed over him. Roman Dalton was a Beast, and the silver bullet that had failed to kill the ex-cop had proved it. A normal man would have been splattered all over the sidewalk from that sniper shoot, but Dalton was a monster. He was a man who was more than just a man.

So many preparations to make, and the horrid man had so little time.

I awoke in mind-numbing pain, which was an improvement over the brain-shattering agony from earlier. Looking around, I could see I was in the state-of-the-art operating room of Doctor Frankenstein. Well, state-of-the-art 1940s operating room of Doctor Frankenstein. The doc didn't like modern equipment. He hated all of the lights and beeps. He was the hands-on type.

"I see you've rejoined the world of the living, Dalton," Frankenstein said from behind his operating mask. Frankenstein was a crime doctor and a very good one. He took care of the underworld and it took care of him. No one really knows the

old coot's true name or story. Hell, no one ever saw him outside
of his scrubs and mask, let alone had a personal conversation
with him. There are very dark stories about his experiments and
tastes, but they've always been performed on scum supplied him
by his clients. The day he touches an innocent is the day we'll
dance. "If you hadn't wakened, I thought I might have that werewolf I've always wanted to play with."

"Not this time, Doc, but who knows what might happen in
the future."

"I'm patient," he said.

My skin was starting to itch with the desire to make blood
come rushing from his lips. I took a second to calm the beast
before continuing. "What happened to me?"

Frankenstein held up a silver bullet. It was an ugly bastard
and covered in my blood. "It appears you have a friend."

"Friends usually buy me drinks, Doc."

"I think he's right, Roman," Duffy chimed in from the corner
of the room where he'd been standing. He'd never liked the doc.
There was bad blood there that no one will spill a word on. I
know, I've asked.

"He's your friend because he only put one of these in you."
Frankenstein laughed as he dripped the slug back onto a metal
table nearby. "If he wanted you dead, he just needs to put one or
two more into you."

"This guy who shot you knows what you are," Duffy said as I
sat up on the table. I could already feel the wound slowly knitting
itself back together. One of the perks of lycanthropy is a rock-
solid constitution.

"I guess we need to find out what he really wants."

Only one more night until the full moon, and the horrid
man could barely contain the excitement that burned red-hot

throughout his body. He was constantly aroused and felt the bloodlust surging, but he knew his patience would be rewarded. He stared longingly at the unconscious woman who lay bound on the floor. He really wanted to taste her blood and feel her flesh rolling around his tongue, but he couldn't stand doing her as a faux wolf. Shortly he would join the other Beasts and eat his fill as a true creature of the night.

I stood over the spot where that bastard shot me. He policed his own brass and cleaned up after himself. He even sprayed a fine mist of bleach and deer urine across every surface to eradicate his scent markers. Maybe a simple dog could be fooled by this, but not me. No one but a wolf could understand the complexity or access to the world of smell we have. My senses were growing stronger the closer we got to the full moon. I couldn't track him through the city yet, but I would when the goddess moon rose.

There will be blood to pay and I will collect all I'm due.

The rest of the day I spent at Duffy's, kissing the green fairy full on her goddamn lips. It was stupid to get so loaded when a hunter was looking for me, but I'm a weak man and this asshole doesn't want me dead. How could a mere human pose the least threat to me when the beast is about ready to break free?

"I think you've had enough today, Roman," Duffy said as he started to slide my emerald bitch-wife away. I grabbed his hand around the bottle and squeezed enough to get his attention.

"I'm convalescing."

He let go with a shrug. "I did my duty; you're on your own."

I was about to say something witty and urban when a regular walked into the bar. It wasn't Hooker Tom who got my attention, but the scent that wafted in with him from the outside.

"What's got your attention?" Duffy asked as I slid the bottle back at him.

"Keep my girlfriend company and don't let any of these other bastards pick her up," I snorted as I charged out into the cold night.

A sniff told me that son-of-a-bitch was down the alley, and I stormed in with a truckload of bravado and a gun waiting to deliver its hot valentines.

A burst of something dusty hit me in the face, and I coughed like I wanted to see what my insides would look like spread across the sidewalk. I looked up from where I had fallen to my knees and saw this horrid little man through my watering eyes. He was holding a fire extinguisher in one hand and a baseball bat in the other. I looked up at him with a questioning stare since my throat no longer worked.

"Silver nitrate particles and pulverized wolf's bane," was all he said.

Werewolf mace, the fucker had created werewolf mace.

He smiled once before kissing me goodnight with his Louisville slugger.

I was growing really tired of waking up in pain, and prying my blood-encrusted eyes open was difficult since my hands seemed to be chained. It took all of two seconds before I realized my skin was burning from where the chains touched my naked flesh. The little sod had used silver chains bolted to the wood floor to restrain my arms and legs. Funny things, you always see the hero using a silver bullet to kill the werewolf in the movies. You might not have realized that the crap still hurts us in human form. Aside from, say, getting shot in the heart with it.

I found this out by accident one day not too long after my first transformation. I was feeling very horny one day and decided to take Pamela Pink up on her offer "ta do me fer free" one day. We were banging away with her on top when I noticed the flash of silver between her ample pale breasts. I was preoccupied at the time and rolled her over for my finishing move, and doggie style is too easy of a joke. I lay full on her chest to get a better angle with that fucking silver cross adhered itself to my chest. My scream was not my finishing move, but it was for her, and she stormed out of my apartment naked and calling me the most creative of names. I was frightened that it was the cross that did it. God was real and pissed at my obviously hell-bound soul.

I later found out it was not the cross when I picked up a silver picture frame in one of the shops.

I'm not allowed back there ever again.

Looking around the room, after ten minutes of crying had allowed me to compartmentalize at least some of the pain, I saw several poster-sized prints of horrific murder scenes similar to the runaway girl from the other day. Actually, this twisted fucker had one of her also. They hung about the large loft room like jerseys hung in the rafters of some pathetic sports arena. Trophies of his black desires. I was so going to enjoy looking through his entrails to see if the black cinder of his soul was hiding there.

Lying on the floor was an unmoving girl around fifteen years old. She was as naked as I was and in a terrible state. She had been violated violently, and her soulless eyes showed that she wasn't coming back. He'd destroyed her mind, and I suspected he had worse plans for her body. A creaking behind me caused me to bolt around despite the renewed searing burn of the chains.

The horrid little man walked into the room naked also. His pale, pimpled skin was slick with sweat. His toenails were of various lengths and thick, yellowed, and crusted. His fat was distributed across his body with all of the care of a farmer throwing shit into his field to fertilize it. His back hair was patchy at best and made him look even greasier and unhealthy.

I looked at his piggy eyes, and they were hungry as he looked back. He kicked the unresponsive girl on the ground once and giggled a girlish squeal.

He was a blemish on life and I was eager to pop him.

"It's almost time," he said as he glanced up at the large skylight. I looked up too and could just see the glimmer of moonrise. It finally dawned on me what this was all about. I may not be the brightest bulb in the room at times; being a werewolf has done nothing to improve that.

"You want the curse?" I croaked, my throat still raw from the dusting.

"Curse?" He screeched as he charged to within three feet of me. I made a lunge, but he knew the length the chains would allow me. "What a dumb animal you truly are."

"You are what you eat, and I eat an awful lot of assholes like you." I grinned my most evil non-canine grin. "You look like greasy chicken to me."

"You get to taste me soon enough."

"Well, that sounds like you fancy me? Are you a fancy boy looking for a bit of fluff?" I said as an angry flush engulf his quivering flesh, and it was as unpleasant to watch as it was to describe.

"Don't push me, Dalton; I wouldn't want to make someone like me angry."

"Noted, but you remind me of something." The piggish thug wasn't biting. "I'm thinking about when my dad would take me to football matches."

"What are you talking about?" the horrid little man said when curiosity finally won out.

"I was always a hungry bastard and he would buy me tons of snacks."

"So?"

"My favorite snack was the bags of peanuts they sold. You ever had those?"

"I didn't like sports then and I don't tolerate them now."

"Big surprise," I said. "I only bring it up because it looks like you're sporting three peanuts there."

The horrid man looked down at his groin and screamed. He looked like he wanted to beat me to death with his fist, and that was fine with me. He'd have to touch me, and mother moon was almost there.

A calmness washed over him and that surprised me. He picked a knife off the floor from behind the prone girl and gave a nasty slash to her thigh. This produced no reaction from her, and I knew my guess about her mental state was completely true.

"I'll just give her your pain; she won't mind."

My angry scream turned into an anguished howl. Silver moonlight kissed me and I changed.

The beast is always prowling behind my eyes. I can feel him moving, snarling, and evaluating every situation I get into. I feel his need to break free and his power every second of my life. People think I'm a drunken fool and I'll die an alcoholic bum. I drink to calm the beast. Three days of the month I drink the moon to release the beast.

"Damn my soul, you are a beautiful bastard," the horrid man said as he took his werewolf mace from the corner of the room and hosed me down.

That was his first mistake.

My wolf form is more powerful than my human form could ever be, no matter what time of the month. The dusting was irritating, but no more incapacitating than if this fool had punched me in the snout. I gave a little snort before locking eyes with this delicious-looking turd. I shook my fur and the dust flew off like water. That's when I smelt the heady aroma of fear wafting off my captor. I stretched my arms out a little and the chains snapped. I looked down, surprised, because there is no way I could have snapped silver chains. I was too weak from the silver poisoning to be that strong yet.

Looking at the ends of the chain, I could see his second mistake. The insides were steel and not silver. The cheap bastard had silver-coated steel chains. I couldn't break them as a human, but they had proved fragile enough as a werewolf.

I needn't tell you his third and last mistake was pissing me off.

I was across the room and on top of the fucker before he could even form the thought to run.

"DO IT!" he screamed up at me. "Bite me and make me a beast like you! I want it! I need it!"

The beast was screaming for his flesh and it took every ounce of control and willpower to leash those demands. Instead of ripping him into small chewable pieces, I head-butted him into unconsciousness. His broken nose leaked like a sieve and I couldn't resist licking it up. Shoot me.

Walking over to the girl, I cut her restraints with a razor-sharp claw. I was wrong about her being forever lost in her happy place. She quickly sat up and whimpered in fear of me.

"Run," was the best I could force out of my canine-like throat. Have you ever seen those cute videos on the web where dogs croak out sounds that sound like "I love you"? It isn't cute at all when a werewolf talks. She ran naked out into the night.

Loping over to that prone fucker, I threw him over my shoulder and headed out after her.

"He'll be awake shortly," Frankenstein said with unbridled glee. "Roman, I cannot thank you enough."

"Where am I?" the horrid little man slurred as he awoke from his drug-induced sleep. "What's happening?"

"You should have the honor of explaining."

"Why, thank you, Doc," I said as I moved over into the pig's line of sight. "You've had a long night."

"What did you do?" the horrid man demanded as he blinked his eyes against the sunlight that streamed into the antique operating theater.

"Well, as you may have guessed, it's daytime and you haven't been bitten by the wolf. At least, not yet." I laughed as I pulled the sheet off the little turd. His eyes grew wide as he saw what had been done to him. "We had to do some prep work first."

He screamed loud and hard at the sight. I waited until he exhausted himself before continuing on.

"Doctor Frankenstein has always wanted a werewolf of his own to explore."

"Indeed, I have."

"However, I figure that a rotten piece of shit like you also needed a bit of karmic retribution," I said as I gave the bloody sutures of one of his four stumps a tweak. "So I asked the doc to take off all of your pesky limbs."

"Nooooooo!"

"If I had bitten you first, you might have grown back those arms and legs. This way, you'll just be a wolf in a box."

"My wolf in the box," Frankenstein said in a tone that even sent a chill down my jaded little spine.

"I'll come back tonight and give you that curse you were so desperate to get, and you should change on the final night tomorrow evening."

"Why?" The horrid little man asked weakly. "Why couldn't you just have done what I asked?"

"You just don't get it, do you?" I asked as I leaned in. "I hate you."

"We will have such a good time learning together," Doctor Frankenstein said as he clapped his hands together.

"See, the doc here wants to learn all of those werewolf secrets, and he's promised to share them with me." I smiled and turned to Frankenstein. "Of course, I'll have to pay him a special visit if he feels the need to share my secrets with the rest of his clientele."

"Perish the thought, Roman," Frankenstein said with an almost sincere tone.

"Any way, I'm going to run out and quench my incredible thirst. Don't fret; I'll be back before moonrise tonight," I said before leaving the herbalist shop that Frankenstein uses as a front for his doc-shop. Duffy sat in his cab waiting for me again.

Damn, I can't forget to ask him how he does that.

———

Artist, sculptor, writer, and filmmaker—*John Donald Carlucci* tries his best to re-create the odd and weird things that move in the dark corners of his imagination. He's spent years publishing pulp magazines, developing his assemblage artwork, and writing his horror and crime noir stories in various media. Find him at johndonaldcarlucci.com.

A FIRE IN THE BLOOD

KATHERINE TOMLINSON

The man slept but the wolf dreamed.
The wolf dreamt of blood and fire.
In its dreams, the wolf ran wild, free of its human cage.
In its dreams there was no past, no future, only the now.
There was no regret, no sorrow, no shame.
There was scent and sensation, food and heat, blood and fire.
The wolf dreamt, but it was the man who woke with the taste
of copper in his mouth and the salt-slick of sweat upon his hairless
skin.

Having the same fucking nightmare every fucking night was
getting old. It was dark moon, so the wolf should have been slum-
bering like a suckling pup, not rampaging through my psyche
night after night.

The wolf was sick and I was dying.

I sat up and fumbled for my cigarettes. Half an hour later I was out of smokes and no sleepier than I'd been when I got up.

I headed over to Duffy's. If I couldn't sleep, I could at least drink.

The only customer in the place was the barfly we called the Professor. Word was he'd once taught philosophy at the university. Now he challenged fellow patrons to trivia contests for beer money.

Most of the time we let him win.

The Professor looked at me out of the one eye that was still open and announced, "You look like shit," when I slid onto a bar stool next to him.

I couldn't disagree.

Duffy didn't bother to chime in with his opinion; he just pulled out an almost-clean glass and drowned a single ice cube in a triple shot of Wild Turkey.

"The nightmare again?" he asked, sliding the drink to a stop in front of me without spilling a drop.

I just gave him a look as I drained the glass.

Duffy poured me another.

"You know," the Professor said, "The origin of the phrase 'nightmare' is actually pretty interesting."

"Jesus," Duffy swore under his breath.

"Buy you a drink, Professor?" I asked to short-circuit the lecture.

He paused in mid-sentence, delighted by the offer.

"That's very kind of you, Roman," he said.

"I'll have what he's having," he said to Duffy.

Duffy raised his eyebrows but poured the drink without comment.

"To your very good health," the Professor toasted, slamming the liquor without ceremony.

Duffy motioned with the bottle and I nodded for him to top me off.

He leaned toward my glass but stopped short with the bottle poised above it, staring into my face with unusual intensity.

"What?" I asked.

"You're bleeding," he said and handed me a napkin.

I looked into the mirror on the back bar and saw a thick trail of dark blood snaking down from my left nostril.

That's new, I thought.

"What you need is some lemon and salt," the Professor said.

"I'm not making him a fucking margarita," Duffy said.

"To stop the bleeding," the Professor said. "Tip your head back, Roman," he instructed, "try to breathe through your mouth."

I ignored both of them, pinching the bridge of my nose to stop the flow.

Duffy peered at me closely.

"Maybe it's time to see a doctor," he suggested.

"You gonna foot the bill?" I asked. I was operating on financial triage these days; money for doctors wasn't even close to the top of my list.

"Maybe you should see a priest," the Professor said.

"Why would I want to do that?" I snapped. The question came out in a wolf's snarl, and the Professor cringed away from me.

Shit.

"Just, you know, a priest might be able to help you," the Professor said meekly. "Lay his healing hands on you."

"Pour him another," I said to Duffy, feeling guilty.

The Professor drank his whiskey. "Cheers," he said, but he avoided my eyes as he said it and left soon after.

I didn't have the money to go to a doctor and I didn't have

the faith to go to a priest, so I split the difference and went to see Quinver.

He creeps me out, but Quinver's the only one in The City who might have a clue about what's going on with me.

The sign on his office door says he's a chiropractor and during the day, that's how he earns his living. The nights, though, the nights are a different story.

Rumor has it he's a necromancer, or worse, and that what he gets up to at night is not something you want to know about.

The truth is a little more complicated, but suffice it to say, you don't want to get on his bad side. In the wrong frame of mind, Quinver can kill you just as easily as he can cure you.

I knew he'd still be at his office. Quinver keeps odd hours.

"What do you want, Roman?" he asked when he looked up from his laptop and saw me standing in the doorway of his examining room. "I'm busy."

Quinver doesn't like me, so that cuts down on the small talk. He also knows what I am, so that eliminates the need for context.

"I've been having nightmares," I said without preamble. "Dreams of fire and blood."

That got his attention. "Wolf dreams?"

I nodded.

He closed his laptop and stared at me thoughtfully.

"Have you seen her in your dreams?" he asked.

Her?

"A woman?"

He shook his head. "Not a woman."

Quinver being cryptic meant he was scared of something. That scared me.

Quinver isn't afraid of anything living and few things dead.

"No," I said.

"Sit down and take off your coat," he ordered, rummaging in a drawer for a needle and some vacuum tubes.

"Roll up your sleeve."

Neither of us said anything during the half-hour it took for my sluggish blood to fill three vials.

When he finished with the procedure, Quinver left the room without explanation.

He came back a few minutes later, a smear of blood around his mouth.

Instead of sitting back down on his stool, he remained standing, as if ready to flee at any moment.

I did not take that as a good sign.

"It's not voodoo," he said finally, which was a relief.

I'd been sure one of the Haitians had put a curse on me, sending me a nasty little message that might not kill me but would keep me out of action for a good long time.

"Don't be too happy about it," he said. "It's a summoning."

A summoning?

"That's going to a lot of trouble just to get in touch with me," I said, trying to lighten the mood. "They could just ring me," I added. "I'm in the book."

Quinver didn't crack a smile.

"So who is it?" I asked.

"Not who, what," he replied.

"What?" I asked impatiently.

"She's called Azar," he said, and hesitated before adding, "she's a Persian fire demon."

Of course she is.

"We're a long way from the Middle East," I said. "What does a Persian fire demon want with a werewolf?"

"Nothing good."

I waited for him to say something else. *Like fucking pulling teeth*, I thought.

"Not just you," he finally said, "or rather, not you in any specific way. She's looking for all the werewolves in the city."

Again, I had to practically beg for the rest of it.

"Why?"

He sighed. "You really ought to read a book occasionally," he said. "Especially with the kinds of cases you've been getting."

He fell silent again, for so long I wondered if he really wasn't going to tell me anything else.

"She's raising an army," he said. "Gathering conscripts from among the wolfen."

Quinver is the only one I know who uses the old term for my kind.

"That doesn't make sense," I said. "What could she possibly offer us?"

"Transformation," he said. "Apotheosis. Transcendence."

He saw my puzzlement.

"She's going to turn you all into fire wolves and use your blood to breed demons. And then she's going to unleash apocalypse."

Apocalypse. That I understood.

"You know Zef?" Quinver asked.

Jozef Bejko was a moon-faced Albanian, the alpha of a pack that was into human trafficking, computer hacking, and arms dealing. They weren't a nice crew, and Zef was the worst of them. He'd killed the previous alpha in human form, beating the wolf to death with fists the size of waffle irons.

"I know Zef," I said.

"His whole pack disappeared a week ago."

"All of them?"

He nodded grimly. "You need to prepare," he said. "The headaches and the fevers and the nightmares and the bleeding—those are symptoms that you're being summoned."

"Let me guess," I said. "Resistance is futile."

A look of annoyance crossed his face. He jammed his hands into the pockets of his lab coat, but not before I saw they were trembling.

"You need to prepare yourself," he said again. "Sooner or later Azar will get tired of waiting for you to come to her, and she'll come to you. When that happens, it'll be too late for making plans."

Quinver has a crap bedside manner.

"You should leave town," Ivan said when he came into Duffy's at the end of his shift.

"You're not the one having the nightmares," I said. "If I don't deal with this, it's only going to get worse."

I knocked back my drink.

"And I'm not sure I can deal with worse."

Ivan gave me a look and finished his coffee.

"Your funeral," he said, which maybe wasn't the best thing to say under the circumstances.

"Fuck," he said as he signaled for another coffee. "You're bleeding again."

"I rest my case," I said as I stuffed a napkin up my nose.

Ivan seemed to come to a decision.

"Okay," he said.

"Okay?" I asked.

"About a month ago, right around the time you started having your dreams, a woman checked into the Sea Mist Hotel."

I knew the place, a no-tell motel catering to sailors and prostitutes. It had burned down three weeks earlier under suspicious circumstances.

"She wasn't the usual pay-as-you-go skank," Ivan said, "and that attracted attention."

"Never a good thing in that part of town," Duffy interjected.

"Tell me about the fire," I said.

"You've heard this story?" Ivan asked with a smirk.

"I've heard the rumors," I said.

Ivan shook his head. "Rumors," he said, and took a breath. "The story we got from the concierge is that a sailor from Kazakhstan wouldn't take no for an answer and broke into the lady's room after she'd retired for the night. The screaming started a few minutes later."

Ivan paused to take a slurp of his coffee, knowing that we were hanging on his words. Man knows how to tell a story, I'll give him that.

"They weren't a woman's screams. Half an hour later, all that was left of the hotel was the foundation. We found his skeleton in the rubble of what used to be a guest room."

"And the woman?" the Professor asked.

"Gone like smoke in the wind."

The Professor was wide-eyed.

"Until three days ago, when she showed up at the Pink Pussy," Ivan added.

"Looking for a job?" Duffy asked.

Ivan watched my face as he got to the last bit. "Looking for a piece of Albanian donkey shit."

"Zef?" I asked.

He nodded. "I don't know what this Azar is," Ivan said, "but she is double the worst trouble you've ever been in.

"Shame on you, Detective Walker," said a woman whose voice was like burnt honey. "Talking trash about someone you've never even met."

Ivan whirled around, his hand going to his gun.

The woman wasn't even looking at him; her black eyes were boring into mine.

"Roman Dalton," she said, "I've been looking for you."

Lucky me, I thought.

Ivan took a step toward her then stopped as if hitting a barrier. He stood there, looming over her. Slender as he is, he probably outweighed Azar by a hundred pounds. She wasn't intimidated in the least.

Bad things come in small packages, I thought.

She was ugly as homemade sin but carried herself like a beauty queen.

On first glance, she looked utterly harmless, but a second look showed there was something…off…about her.

Even drunk as I was, I was afraid.

She looked past me to Duffy, who looked ready to piss his pants.

"What do you want?" I asked her.

She gave me her full attention then and smiled. "World peace," she said and laughed. "An end to global warming."

She leaned closer to me, her scent an intoxicating blend of spice and sex. Up close I could see the dark pools of fire in her eyes where the pupil should have been.

Her hot breath touched my face and I felt a chill.

Despite myself, I shrank back.

That made her chuckle again.

"I don't want you," she whispered into my ear, "I want the wolf."

"You can have it," I said before I thought, for I never wanted the wolf in the first place.

"Thank you," she said, and kissed me as if trying to suck out my soul.

Even as my mind cringed, my body reacted.

There was a fire running through my veins.

I was burning up.

An orgasm shuddered through me at her touch.

"Get away from him," someone yelled, and I turned my head to see that Ivan had drawn his gun and was pointing it at her.

She flicked a graceful hand in his direction. "Leave us," she said and he was knocked off his feet. He fired as he fell.

The shots went through her body as if she were made of smoke, the bullets burrowing into the bar, narrowly missing the Professor, who was too drunk to react.

"Stop," Ivan ordered, lurching to his feet and lumbering toward us in what seemed like slow motion.

I couldn't move, couldn't even catch my breath.

She gestured, and suddenly the scar on Ivan's neck caught fire.

The flames peeled away from the scar and ran across his throat like a fiery garrote. Azar moved her fingers and uttered a curse, and the flame tightened around his neck, strangling and burning him at the same time.

Duffy grabbed a seltzer bottle, but before he could spray it, Azar glanced in his direction and with another word, sent him flying into the back bar so hard the mirror shattered.

"That's seven years of bad luck," she said with a sneer. "If you live that long."

Dismissing Duffy, she turned back to watch Ivan, who was gagging and clawing at his neck as the fire chewed through his flesh.

Moments later, he collapsed at her feet and lay still.

"No," I blurted out, horrified.

She turned back to me.

"What the hell are you?" I asked.

"I am what I am," she said, with another eerie smile. "There is no way you can comprehend my awesomeness."

"Try me," I said. "Explain yourself. Explicate the many ways in which you are divine." I wanted to know, yes, but I also wanted to delay whatever was coming next. I'm no psychic but I knew it was going to be bad.

Instead of answering, she uttered three more words and ripped away my vulpine self, tearing it free of my body like she was deboning a fish.

It hurt like a motherfucker.

I awoke screaming from a dream of blood and death to find a ghastly-looking Ivan Walker standing beside my hospital bed. His hands were bandaged, but the burn mark across his throat was red and raw and seeping. It looked painful.

The sight brought me back to the night after I'd met my wolf and had awakened in the hospital to find Walker eating grapes and playing Sudoku.

Now he was the one who looked like death warmed over.

"You're alive," I said, surprised.

"No thanks to you," he said, his voice raspier than usual. The burn on his neck moved in synch with his words, almost like a second mouth.

The hospital room was freezing. It had been a long time since I'd been this cold. The wolf's body temperature ranged four degrees higher than my human one, and I'd grown used to warming myself at the wolf's internal fire.

But now the wolf was gone. She'd taken it from me.

I should have felt liberated, but instead I felt sick.

"What happened?" I asked.

"She took your wolf," Ivan said, "then she set the bar on fire."

"Taking the wolf was a favor," I said, not sounding remotely convincing, even to myself.

"That depends on your definition of favor," Ivan said and looked out the window before he continued.

"The wolf didn't come clean, Roman. Your soul came with it."

My soul? Who are you and what have you done with Ivan?

He didn't like my reaction.

"I saw it, Roman," he said. "The wolf was wearing your soul around his neck like a charm."

I dismissed the topic with a wave of my hand and fought back the nausea even that simple gesture caused.

Not good. Not good at all.

"Anybody hurt in the fire?"

"The Professor's next door," Ivan said, "recovering from smoke inhalation. Duffy will have to close for a few days to repaint but the fire was mostly for show."

He unconsciously touched the wound on his neck. That hadn't been for show.

It had been a mistake for Azar to leave Ivan alive.

Hubris.

I could use that.

"Where's Azar now?" I asked Ivan.

"We're looking for her."

"She's not going to be hard to find," Quinver said from the doorway.

He strode over to my bed and immediately began unpacking thermoses and plastic bags from a tattered messenger bag with the logo of a long-defunct pharmaceutical company.

As he measured and poured and swirled and mixed liquids from one container to another, an unpleasant odor combined of fungi, wet dog, and eucalyptus filled the air.

He decanted a dark green liquid into a small glass bottle that had once held iced tea.

"Take this," he ordered. "It's better if you drink it fast."

He wasn't kidding.

"God, that tastes fucking awful," I said.

"Don't be such a baby," he said.

"It's three days until the full moon," I said, locking eyes with my visitor.

"I know," he said.

"What happens then?" Ivan asked. "Without the wolf?"

"If he and the wolf aren't re-integrated before the full moon, Roman will die," Quinver said.

Ivan looked at me. "That's true?"

"I've lived with the wolf too long," I explained. "When the moon is full, my body will still respond to the call. It'll warp and twist itself inside out without any wolfskin to protect it. I won't be able to survive that way, and I won't be able to change back."

The room was silent for a moment.

Ivan turned to Quinver.

"Isn't there anything you can do?"

"Maybe," he said. "I need to do some research."

And with that he turned and left the room.

"That fucking guy," Ivan said.

I knew what he meant.

"See you later," Ivan said, and then he was gone, too.

About an hour later I was sent home with an admonition to avoid any strenuous activity and to drink plenty of liquids.

They weren't specific about what sort of liquids, so I used my own judgment.

At some point later I fell into a dreamless sleep that was more like a coma.

While I slept, Azar bore the first of her werewolf-demon hybrids, and their birthpangs ushered in a taste of what was to come.

Whole blocks of buildings burned to the street, leaving behind only blackened beams and scorched stone. There was no question of the fires being of natural origin; witnesses spoke of seeing green and purple flames twisting around each other in the inferno. Some spoke of creatures seen in the fire's shadows.

Fear floated like ashes in the air.

The destruction was wanton and random, as cruel as it was pointless.

Azar had simply wanted to announce her presence and demonstrate her power in celebration of the births.

The mayor left town. He didn't want to stick around for whatever she had in mind for Act Two.

Those who could afford to do so followed his lead.

I wish I'd had that option.

I was working up the energy to brew a pot of coffee when there was a knock at my door. I opened it to find Zef standing there.

He saw my shock. "The rumors of my death have been greatly exaggerated," he said.

"Wishful thinking," I replied, but I stood aside to let him in.

"Coffee?" I offered.

"Something stronger?" he countered and I obliged, dividing what was left of my bottle from the night before. "Shëndeti tuaj," he said, and drank up.

Finished, he let his eyes wander around the room appraisingly.

"You live in a shit hole," he observed.

"Then you should feel right at home," I countered.

He bared his teeth at me in a semblance of a smile and slammed his empty glass on my coffee table so hard something broke.

"I heard about your pack," I said. "She has all of them?"

"All of them," he said. "Including Arjana."

His mate.

"None of them survived the transformation," he added. "I found their bodies discarded like used condoms."

Jesus.

"How did you escape?" I asked and he growled.

"I was out of town," he said finally, his voice tinged with grief and loss and anger. There was lots of anger.

"Quinver says there's a way we can help each other." He looked at me expectantly.

So nice of Quinver to ask me first.

"I'm listening," I said, knowing already I wasn't going to like whatever he'd come to tell me.

Over the next hour, Zef explained what he had in mind. He and I and Quinver would travel to the park Azar was using as her base of operations. Once we were there, Quinver would dose me with a psychotropic to literally "free my mind."

In wolf form, Zef would then bite me, and my consciousness would fill his mind like wine being decanted into crystal.

"And then what?" I asked, horrified at the prospect of such mental intimacy.

"Then we find your wolf and kill it so the spirit can go back into you."

"That seems pretty complicated."

He studied my face, searching for something he wasn't seeing. "It's simple," he said, "if you're not afraid."

Of course I'm afraid, you fucking douche.

"You can shift even when the moon isn't full?" I asked him.

"I can shift whenever I want," he said. "I can show you if you like."

That was interesting. Someone like Zef didn't offer to share anything unless he absolutely had no choice.

"And when I'm whole again?" I asked. "What happens then?"

"Then we hunt. We kill the fire-bitch's spawn and then we quench her fire in our blood."

Easier said than done.

"And Quinver signed off on this?"

"He says our chances of success are not good but that we have to try."

Well, hell, why didn't you say so?

"Sounds like a plan," I lied.

It was after midnight when we met at the park, but we had no trouble finding our way. Azar had surrounded her new domain with a 12-foot barrier of flames. It was an intimidating sight.

We stopped in the shadow of the wall. Zef gazed at the flaming fence with contempt.

"Stage dressing," he said. "Special effects."

There a reason he's an alpha. I couldn't even fake that kind of courage.

Quinver pulled a thermos out of his messenger bag and handed it to me.

"Drink it all," he instructed.

I took a tentative swallow. The liquid was fizzy and sweet, but thick.

I drank it quickly and belched.

I almost laughed until I realized I could see it—the color and shape of the burp.

"Synesthesia," Quinver explained. "It's normal."

Beside me, Zef growled. I turned to face the biggest wolf I'd ever seen. Before I could register the sheer size of him, he bit me in the throat.

I felt his teeth slice into my flesh, tearing through muscle and crunching into tendon and bone.

I blacked out and when I came to, my body was on the ground and I was looking out of the wolf's eyes.

The first time I was bitten, I'd first thought it was a bad dream, a drunkard's fantasy. This time I didn't have the comfort of delusion or illusion. I knew exactly what was going on.

I fought off a wave of vertigo.

A wolf thought came to me.

Let us hunt, brother.

And we ran, straight through the wall of flames.

Where is your wolf?

I let my senses settle, then cast them out until I felt a familiar presence just at the edge of our shared consciousness.

Near the fountain.

We see.

Zef covered the distance fast, barreling into the group of wolves surrounding the fountain and knocking Roman-wolf off its feet.

The wolf flattened its ears in fear, rolling over to show its belly. Zef-wolf stood over it, establishing dominance as the other wolves slunk away. Then Zef-wolf transformed into a man and began to batter the Roman-wolf into bloody submission with his bare fists.

No!

Stop!

Zef ignored me as he gathered the beaten animal in his arms and ran with it through the flames. I fought to get free of the bone cage of Zef's skull, but I was a helpless passenger, trapped in his mind, along for the ride.

The fire had not burned the wolf going in, but as he passed through it in human form, I felt Zef's skin scorch as the flames caressed him.

As strong as he was, he was gasping by the time he reached Quinver.

He dumped the unconscious wolf next to my body. "Now," he said, and Quinver pulled out a set of silver daggers and plunged them into the Roman-beast's heart.

I felt it die.

It was not an easy death.

Working quickly, Quinver skinned its pelt and draped it over my body.

"Now," Zef said again and I felt my consciousness eject from his and slam back into my own body.

I howled in agony and the Roman-wolf joined me, bonding to me, blood and bone and soul.

I turned over and vomited, gulping in deep breaths until my vision cleared and my stomach settled.

Quinver gave me water and I drank thirstily.

I could hear the fire wolves howling behind the flaming barrier.

They were howling for our blood. We'd invaded their territory.

She'll know we're coming now, I thought.

Yes, Zef thought back, *she will*.

We looked at each other in surprise, then turned to Quinver. He shrugged.

"The telepathy is a side effect," he said. "It should wear off."

Should? I didn't fancy swimming in Zef's cesspool of a mind a minute longer than I had to.

"How much of this are you making up as we go along?" I asked Quinver.

"I didn't think we'd get this far," he admitted.

We're wasting time, Zef thought impatiently.

"Are you ready?" he asked aloud.

"Be a shame to go home without kicking some ass," I said.

Zef looked at me skeptically, totally unimpressed.

"Let the wolf take over," he said, and I let my mind go blank.

Zef changed then and spoke to my wolf, and just like that, I changed too.

Instinct.

Survival.
Blood.

Our plan was insane, of course. The only advantage we'd ever had was the element of surprise, and that was blown to fuck. We knew the nursery was in the stone folly at the center of the park. It was little more than a gazebo, a circle of columns supporting a domed roof. Azar had chosen the place because nothing there would burn. You can't fight a fire demon with water, you have to quench her fire in blood.

Lots of blood.

The blood of her demon children would do nicely.

Our plan was to kill as many of the fire wolves as we could, starting a backfire that would herd the others toward the stone folly. We would follow the fire and fall upon the new-born creatures, ripping out their throats and flinging their bodies around like fleshy thuribles, spraying their half-wolf blood on Azar.

The demon babies died howling like wolves, hissing like flames, crying like children. But they died.

Azar shrieked her curses and threw her fireballs, made clumsy by the pain of the corrosive blood. As we reached the center of her stone redoubt, a blue-eyed fire wolf jumped in front of Azar to protect her.

I shared Zef's recognition.

Arjana-wolf…

He hesitated but I did not, and the she-wolf died in a frenzy of flaming fur and gnashing teeth. Zef turned on me in a fury and snarled, but his rage was deflected as Azar sent a trio of fire wolves in his direction.

He caught one by the throat and flung it to the floor, then simply galloped through the other two.

Azar stood at the center of the nursery and screamed in rage as we converged on her from two different directions.

Zef reached her first.

Azar threw a blast of fire straight at him, but all that did was ignite his fur and madden him further.

Enemy.

Kill.

I couldn't tell whose thoughts I was hearing, my own or Zef's or the wolves'. It didn't matter. There was only blood. There was only fire.

Zef leapt upon Azar, knocking her on her back and setting her garments on fire. He mounted her in wolf form, pinning her down with his massive paws, his claws nailing her to the stone. He changed back to human midway through the rape, but did not disengage from her.

A black fire rose from Azar's body like a demented aura, but he held on. Her blood hissed on his burning skin as he buried his human teeth in her flesh and began to feast.

Fat dripping from his burning body fueled the black fire as it consumed them both. The remaining wolves backed off, as any animal will back away from fire.

His last thought was human.

Arjana.

And then there was nothing but an evil smell rising in the heated air and the crackling of the dying flames.

The last of her creatures died with her—the fire wolves withering, the demon children dissolving into toxic pools of burning blood.

I walked away from the park and found Quinver where we'd left him, sitting as calmly as if what had happened had only been a particularly vivid 3-D movie he'd been watching.

If he was surprised that Zef hadn't returned with me, he

didn't show it.

That pissed me off. Zef and I had been connected as he died, and some of his agony had transferred to me.

Quinver gathered up his jars and his herbs and packed everything away in his ratty messenger bag.

"Come on," he said, "I'll buy you a drink."

We walked back into The City as the trails of fire burned a path straight through to the sea where the salty water, so much like blood, finally extinguished them.

When the ashes cooled, superstitious survivors seeded the burnt ground with protective charms and chanted prayers and offered up hymns.

The mayor returned and issued a decree turning the stone folly in the park into a memorial for those who'd died.

Made me want to sneak out there one night with a sledgehammer.

Ivan later told me the police had found the body of Zef's wife lying peacefully in the bedroom of the penthouse he owned. Her body had been wrapped in velvet and covered in gold jewelry and flowers, with a love note placed in her mouth.

An autopsy showed Arjana had indeed died from the trauma of her separation. No matter what happened in the park, Zef hadn't planned on coming back because there was nothing for him to return to.

Wolves mate for life.

At night the wolf sleeps, but I am wakeful.

My memories are vivid, and human: the stench of burning flesh, the hot splash of blood, the sight of impossible things that cannot be unseen.

When it gets too bad I climb out of bed and find a bottle.

I pour the whiskey down my throat and feel the fire in my belly.

And then, and only then, and only if I am lucky, will I fall asleep myself.

Katherine Tomlinson is a former reporter who prefers making things up. Her latest collection of short fiction, *L.A. Nocturne II*, was published in March. She is the author of the serial novel *NoHo Noir*, illustrated by Mark Satchwill. Her short fiction has appeared in *A Twist of Noir*, *Shotgun Honey*, *ThugLit*, *Dark Valentine*, *Dark Fire*, *Powder Burn Flash*, and *Luna Station Quarterly*. Read more of her short fiction on her blog, "Kattomic Energy."

BEFORE THE MOON FALLS

PAUL D. BRAZILL

DUFFY AWAKES DROWNING IN SWEAT. Still smothered by bad dreams. Gunshots echo through his brain. Then the sound of helicopter blades. Screams.

It takes him a moment to adjust to the surroundings; the room looks unfamiliar in the wan light. Slowly, his eyes make out the details of his sparse living room. He's on the sofa, tangled up in a worn blanket cradling a bottle of bourbon as if it were a teddy bear. He lies there for a moment, each heartbeat like the tick of a clock, and edges off the sofa. His joints ache as he stumbles to the window and peels back the blinds.

A constellation of streetlights and a galaxy of Christmas decorations fade into the distance towards Banks' Hill. A feral group of Hoodies trudge through the snow. They shuffle through the redbrick Ace of Spades archway and into the narrow alleyway that leads to the rear of Klub Zodiak. More of Dragan's new recruits. More cannon fodder.

Someone, somewhere nearby is whistling Hank William's "I'm So Lonesome I Could Cry." Or maybe he's imagining it.

Duffy shakes his head. He's exhausted. His mind playing tricks on him. His sleep is becoming increasingly fitful these days. Spectral. Like wading through molasses. Guilt, his mother would have said. And she'd be right.

And then Duffy sees him.

Standing in the Zebra Bar's doorway, illuminated by the flash of his Zippo as he lights a cigarette. His face looks pallid. Lips as red as a clown's. He's wearing a long dark raincoat, his hair long and black like rats' tails. A chill slices through Duffy like the ice pick that took out Trotsky.

A black limousine purrs around the corner and stops. Ivan Walker salutes and gets in.

Duffy walks into the bathroom and switches on the shaving lamp. He avoids looking in the mirror, knowing what he'll see: bloodshot eyes; dirty, unshaven face; inky black hair. His skin riddled with acne.

He coughs. Spits. Coughs again. A Rorschach test of blood splashes the white basin. He turns on the tap and tries to wash it away.

A brittle, icy morning and the air tastes like lead. Duffy glides the black BMW through The City's cobbled streets, listening to Bessie Smith's "Downhearted Blues." Eases the car along New World Street, taking in its expensive shops, hotels, cafes, and bars. It feels like the calm before the storm. It is.

A rickshaw pulls up outside the Euro-China Hotel and a couple of drunken Chinese business men tumble out. The rickshaw driver is Travis, a tall blonde Californian surfer girl. She wears a screaming-red chauffeur's uniform and a forced grin. She laughs at something the men say as she clutches the wad of notes one of them hands her. She notices Duffy as he cruises past and taps her chauffeur's cap in a mock salute. He blows her a kiss.

Dragan crouches in the back seat, like a coiled python. He wipes a fleck of cocaine from his nose and sits up. His eyes dance the flamenco. He chuckles, lights a cigar, and gazes out of the window, like a king surveying his domain. Which isn't too far from the truth.

"Why do you always listen to such depressing music, Duffy?" says Dragan.

"Not depressing," says Duffy. "Cathartic. Helps me process the wear and tear of life. Chew it up and spit it out. You should do the same. Listen to a bit of Billie Holliday. 'Lady Day,' as she was known. Would sort you out, no worries."

But Dragan's not listening.

"Remember Richie Sharp?" he asks, gesturing toward Patrick's Irish Pub, which spills out its early morning dregs. Puking and mewling executives. Pumped-up pimps. Hairy-arsed bikers.

"Rings a bell," says Duffy.

"You must remember. The fence. He used to call himself Mr. Google. Said he could find anything for you. Eh? Remember?"

"Yeah," says Duffy. "That flabby farm boy that used to practically live in Patrick's? The shittiest pub in The City, but he loved it."

"Happy days, those, eh? I miss them sometimes. Don't you?'

"Naw. Nostalgia's not what it used to be."

Back in those days, Dragan was just a speed freak. A jumped-up Serbian car thief. A drug dealer with ambitions. There'd been a lot of blood under the bridge since then, thought Duffy. Rivers of the stuff.

"Whatever happened to him, anyway?" he says.

"Fuck knows," says Dragan. "Last time I saw him was well over five years ago. Just after the last wave of refugees swarmed into The City. He had hundreds of them working for him: dealers, whores, pickpockets, hackers, croupiers. I think he was screwing Bronek Malinowski's wife at the time, though. So…"

Duffy laughs.

"Was Sharp the one they roasted in the pizza oven?"

"No, that was the French guy. Journalist. They frizzled him. Who knows what happened to Richie Sharp, though…"

Duffy turns right at the Palm Tree Bar and heads down Othello Avenue, looking up at Rhino Towers, Count Otto Rhino's grey Gothic headquarters, looming over The City like a giant gargoyle keeping danger at bay. Though not exactly doing too good a job of it.

As he turns the corner and heads toward the Central Railway Station, a big black van suddenly screeches in front of him and blocks his way. He brakes, but his reactions are slow and he slams into the side of the van.

"Bollocks," says Duffy.

"What the fuck?" growls Dragan. His eyes bulge out of his head. He grabs his Glock from its shoulder holster and opens the car door.

"Close it and hold on!" Duffy shouts.

He screeches the car into reverse. Dragan falls back in his seat, the door wide open. And then another van turns the corner and slams into the back of Duffy's car, stopping his exit.

Within seconds, a swarm of massive shaven-headed men dressed in military fatigues rush out of the vans. Otto Rhino's Frog Boys.

Dragan slams his door closed. The men start attacking the car with hammers and baseball bats. A giant of a man pulls out a shotgun and blasts the bulletproof windscreen, which cracks like a spiderweb.

"What the fuck is this?" screams Dragan. The cigar falls into his lap.

One of the vans sounds its horn, and within seconds the men rush back inside.

"Who would dare? Who the fuck would dare?"

He sits back, stunned. The dropped cigar burns a hole into his lap. He looks down for a moment and brushes it away as if it is a mosquito.

Dragan slumps in the blood-red leather armchair that is jammed in a darkened corner of the office. A ghost of the man he once was.

"So what's the plan?" says Duffy, flicking through a copy of *National Geographic*.

Dragan grunts. He holds a bottle of red wine in one of his hands. He disinterestedly watches as it drips onto the wooden floorboards.

"There's a rat in the kitchen," he says. "An informer. There's no way that Otto Rhino would come at me like that without information."

At a large desk, Lulu, a tall raven-haired woman, uses a gold credit card to chop up a little heap of cocaine. She leans forward and snorts through an Eiffel Tower souvenir pen.

"*Ay caramba*, motherfucker," she says, her Galway accent as thick and dark as an Irish coffee. She turns to Dragan. "Maybe it's that Haitian guy? Ton Ton Philippe?"

Dragan growls.

Duffy pours himself another large gin and hands the bottle to Lulu.

"Gin makes you sin," she says, with a chuckle. Dragan glares at her as she swigs from the bottle.

She turns away, retouches her makeup in a hand mirror, and stands.

Duffy can see rage rumble inside Dragan like a thundercloud.

Lulu walks over to him. She looks good. She's tall and in her early twenties with wan-looking skin, red lipstick slashed across her full lips, and black hair cut into a bob. She wears a red PVC raincoat and shiny black stiletto heels that click on the floorboards. Dragan takes a wad of cash from his wallet and wearily hands it to her.

"Whatever you can find out, okay?" he says.

"Aye," says Lulu.

"And by whatever means necessary."

She nods. Smiles.

The James Bond theme begins to play and Dragan takes out his mobile phone.

"Yes," he says and listens for a few moments before answering. He slumps over the large oak desk.

"And exactly how much of a bollocks is '*a bit of a bollocks*'?" he asks. His expression is volcanic.

"Maybe I'll go?" says Lulu.

"Not a bad idea," says Duffy.

Dragan waves indifferently toward her and she walks out of the office door, her head held down but still watching. And still listening.

Dragan smashes the bottle on the floor. The red stain crawls into the wood's cracks and crevices. He stands up, lights a cigar, and gazes out the window.

The Old City square is almost empty. Just the occasional little ant scuttling across the snow. Duffy can hear the sound of the music from Klub Zodiak below. He can feel the throb of the bass, thumping its message.

Dragan pulls a bag of cocaine from his desk drawer and trails a line of powder along the window pane.

"I'll be off, then," says Duffy.

Dragan nods slowly.

"And Duffy, remember to watch out for mercenary eyes."

He points a shaking finger and immediately looks more than one thousand years old.

As Duffy blasts Ricardo's brains across the snow-smothered ground, a row of black birds that were lined up on telephone lines like notes on sheet music scatter and slice through the milky whiteness.

Snow dandruffs the corpse as he takes the Glock from Ricardo's hand and pushes it down the back of his jeans. Looking at the fat heap on the ground, his scraggly beard and unkempt hair matted with blood, he is overcome with sadness, guilt. And anger.

"You useless fucker, Ric," he says.

He takes out his hip flask, toasts Ricardo, takes a sip, and pours the rest of the vodka onto the snow.

He grabs the cadaver by the ankles and hauls his massive corpse towards the dilapidated cottage, leaving behind a snaking trail of blood. In front of the door, he pauses and wipes his brow with the blood-stained sleeve of his biker's jacket.

He catches his breath and gazes over at a Christmas tree that is lit up with shimmering, dancing multi-coloured lights. A wind chime that hangs above the door tinkles. He smiles. Elsewhere, for a moment.

Dragan's Harley pulls up outside the cottage. He takes off his black crash helmet and runs a hand through his freshly cropped hair, scratches his head, and dismounts.

"Well?" he says.

Duffy, angry, ignores him. The heavy wooden door creaks as he pushes it open. Ricardo's head bounces off every concrete step as he drags the body downstairs into the dark and dingy basement and onto a sheet of dirty green tarpaulin.

He switches on a lone light bulb, which buzzes and flickers, revealing a room cluttered with wooden barrels. A dirty, cracked mirror hangs precariously above a rusted metal sink.

"So what did he say?" says Dragan, as he pounds down the stairs, the sound of his feet echoing around the basement.

There is a burning in Duffy's chest. He bends forward, grips his knees, and hikes up a wad of bloody phlegm.

"He said nothing."

"He said nothing or that he knew nothing?"

Duffy sighs.

"He said that he knew nothing."

"And you believed him."

"Yes. Until then the stupid fucker grabbed my gun and tried to make a run for it. Shot at me."

Duffy leans against the sink. It creaks and squeals as he turns the rusty tap and releases the shitty brown water. He splashes it on his face.

"The sad fuck had nothing to lose, I suppose," says Dragan, "apart from his balls." He snorts and lights up a large Havana cigar. "Idiot accountant thinks he can rip me off."

"Well, he got away with it for long enough," says Duffy.

"Did anyone see you?' he says, blowing a perfect trio of smoke rings. "Any spies? Any mercenary eyes?"

"Around here? No," Duffy says. "No. There's no one around here."

"Ha! So you say!"

Dragan's increasing paranoia is like a fingernail down a blackboard to Duffy these days. He clenches his fists, digs his nails into his palms.

"We're in the middle of the fucking countryside. On Christmas fucking morning. Who's going to see me? Fucking carol singers?"

"Did he say anything else?" says Dragan. His bullet-hole eyes bore into Duffy and show no amusement.

"Yes. He cried for his mother."

Dragan peels off his boots and black leather jacket and sits cross-legged on the dirty floor. He is wearing a black sleeveless T-shirt depicting Edward Munch's "The Scream," and a pair of expensive denim jeans.

He plucks a bottle of vodka from one of the wooden barrels that cluttered the room. His wedding ring glints as it catches the light.

"You know what I mean. Did he say anything about Rhino? About Ton Ton Philippe?"

"Ton Ton Philippe…Jesus…that's all you talk about. I told you. He's just a bogey man. A legend that those Haitian mobsters use to keep their protection racket running."

Dragan turns. His face as expressionless a Golem. He pours large measures of vodka into two pink plastic tumblers.

"Well?" says Dragan

"Well, okay," says Duffy. "Well, I'll admit that it was when I mentioned Ton Ton Philippe that he did a runner. But it's all these scare stories. All these voodoo and black magic bullshit rumours that are filling The City."

Dragan looks lost in thought for a moment. He stands motionless, and not for the first time Duffy is reminded of the robot in the film The Day The Earth Stood Still, waiting for a sign from his master. The only noise is the buzz of the light and the sound of Dragan's breathing.

Eventually, he breaks into a smile.

"Well, we'll see," he says.

He walks over to Ricardo's corpse and shakes his head.

"Misguided loyalty, my friend," sighs Dragan.

He passes Duffy a tumbler of vodka.

"Cheers," he says.

"Up yours," says Duffy.

They down the drinks in one.

"Okay, back to work," says Dragan, slamming his tumbler down on the table.

He digs into a darkened corner of the room and pulls out something heavy and metallic.

"I think it's time to sever Mr. Ricardo's contract," smirks Dragan as he starts up the chainsaw.

A sliver of moon garrottes the coal black sky and Duffy's heart pounds as he stands outside Klub Zodiak. Its shimmering and buzzing neon sign is reflected in a pool of blood.

He feels the cold metal in his fist as he slams on the steel door of the nightclub until it creaks open. He pushes his way to the bar, breathing in the scent of cheap aftershave, cigarettes and booze. A sultry femme fatale on a chiaroscuro-lit stage purrs a torch song that roars into the abyss.

"Bourbon," says Arek. Duffy nods, take off his leather jacket, and drapes it over a bar stool.

"Is Dragan here?" he says, downing his drink in one.

"Of course," says Arek. "Where else would he be? He thinks that the moment he sets foot outside he's a dead man. The paranoia is eating him like a cancer."

Duffy turns toward the metal door that leads upstairs to Dragan's office.

"For fuck's sake, yer man's lost the plot, Arek; he's away with the fairies. He's like Hitler in his bunker up there. When was the last time he came out?"

"At Darko's funeral."

"And when was that, for Christ sake?"

"A long time ago," growls Arek, his voice like sandpaper.

"What do you think is happening, Duffy?"

Duffy stuffs a fistful of peanuts in his mouth. Chews. Arek waits.

"It's all that cocaine he hoovers up," Duffy says. "And that new stuff coming in from Greece. He's mixing them. Starting the day with uppers, ending the day with downers. Thinks someone's drugging him, would you believe! And I bet he still doesn't know who it is that's out to assassinate him. 'Mercenary eyes, the streets are full of mercenary eyes,' he says. That pretty little wife of his must be ready to piss off I'm sure. And who can blame her? You should do the same thing before he turns on you."

Arek nods.

"Maybe, maybe," he says, as he pours a large glass of whisky. "But where will I go? And what about you? Where will you go?"

"When is more to the point."

Duffy places a metal briefcase on the Klub Zodiak's marble bar and turns to Arek.

"It's all there," he says. "Do you want to count it?"

"No. He'll probably count it himself, the way he is these days," says Arek.

"Aye," Duffy says.

Duffy shivers as the singer whispers "Gloomy Sunday," as if it is her dying breath.

"Great version," he says. "Best version's by Mel Tormé, though. You know what Tormé's nickname was?"

"The Velvet Fog," says Arek.

"Nice to meet a man with good musical knowledge," says Duffy.

It's already past midnight, but Krystyna could swim all night. She loves the Euro-China Hotel's glass swimming pool and the floor-to-ceiling window that gives such a great view of The City's skyline. High above the squalor, the sin, the vice, it twinkles and shines.

"I'll miss this," she says, as she floats on her back.

She gets out of the pool. Duffy rises from his seat and hands Krystyna the towel.

She looks stunning. A pure albino, with eyes as red as blood.

She dries her iron muscled body and goes into the changing room.

Duffy switches off the lights.

Krystyna comes out of the changing room. She's dressed all in white, as usual. Boots, jeans, sweater as pallid as her skin. She switches on her Nokia.

"Any messages?" says Duffy.

"There were two missed calls from Dragan and three texts from him written in a mad garbled mixture of Serbian, Russian, English and Mandarin."

She hands Duffy the phone and he tries to make sense of Dragan's ramblings.

"Like the last words of Dutch Schulz," he says, and laughs. Krystyna doesn't.

She shivers as she plays with her loosening wedding ring.

"He's close to the edge now," she says. "Maybe the house of cards will tumble down quicker than we'd hoped."

The tall men in the black fedoras and long black overcoats look like shadows as they cut through the snow-smothered Old City Square.

A ghostly spiral of smoke drifts up from the husk of the burnt-out car as Duffy falls to his knees, the low hum that hovers in the distance growing louder. Giovanni stares blankly at him, a red dot in the centre of his forehead. The look of incredulity frozen on his dead face.

Duffy looks up, gasping, as a plane roars overhead. His fingers buzz and tingle, and the sensation spreads through his hands and up his arms. The weight of an elephant is on his chest, and then he feels cold hard metal against his forehead.

"You're fucked, boy," says the tallest man, who crouches down, cradling a high-powered rifle. His vowels are long and elasticated. Stretched all the way from Tennessee to The City. He plucks Duffy's gun from where it had fallen and takes Giovanni's pistol from his corpse.

"Yep. Yer fucked. Fucked up the arse," says the squat Irishman as he presses his Doc Martin boot into Duffy's twisted ankle.

Tears fill his eyes as pain rips through him, but he refuses to give them the satisfaction of hearing him scream. He forces a smile and waits for the day to dissolve into night.

But then a clock begins to chime, loud and cacophonous.

The men look up.

"What the fuck is that?" says the Irishman.

First there are a couple of drops. Then trickles, and then there is a flood until what seems to be hundreds of people spill out over the square, like jackals searching for carrion. The men in the black overcoats put away their guns.

"Later, Duffy," the American says. As they slip through the crowd, approaching sirens scream nearer.

The crowd all head in the same direction. Men, women, children. And out of the milieu a stumpy punk rocker with a tall red mohawk walks toward Duffy, beaming a broken-toothed grin.

Shuffling into the corner of a nearby alleyway, Duffy sits down on the front steps of a butcher's shop. Its rancid smell makes him queasy. He pulls his black woollen hat over his frozen ears and plucks a battered packet of Galois from his jacket pocket. He hands one to the young punk, sweat peeling from his acne-scarred face.

The punk grins

"No thanks," he growls in English, his French accent as thick as treacle. "That shit will kill you." The traces of a grin appear at the corners of his mouth.

"Yeah," says Duffy, "but you've got to die of something."

Duffy coughs and spits on the ground. Takes out his hips flask and drinks its acrid contents. He hands it to the punk, who shakes his head.

"Take care of your body, and it'll take care of you." He snickers like the dog in an old cartoon Duffy used to watch as a kid.

"Thanks for dragging me out of...that lot," Duffy says. Nodding toward the town square. "What exactly was happening? All of those people…. Is it some sort of religious festival?"

The punk smirks.

"Sort of. If you call going to work a religion. It's the start of the next shift at the meat packing factory. These are all factory flats and houses. All owned by Otto Rhino."

Duffy slumps to the ground. Takes a pill from his pocket and pops it. Washes it down with the booze.

"Your body really is your temple, isn't it, Duffy?"

Duffy glares at him.

"Who the hell are you, anyway?" he says.

"Guess," says the punk.

"I have no bloody idea."

"Well, I know all about you, Sergeant Duffy."

Duffy automatically reaches for the Bowie knife that he keeps tucked in his boot. It's gone.

"Who the hell are you?"

The punk steps back and holds up his hands. "Relax! You're safe. Take a chill pill! I was just messing with you. Walker sent me."

He moves closer and places the knife in front of Duffy, along with his wallet.

"I'm Robinson," he says, his accent becoming Scottish. "Oliver Beacock Robinson."

"The Magician?"

"Well, I'm no Harry Houdini, but, yeah, that's what they call me."

Duffy remembers the war stories about Robinson during Desert Wave. He was a legend. He could slip undercover, undetected, everywhere. Anywhere. And he was never caught. Lucky bastard, he thinks.

"I thought you'd be...cleaner," says Duffy.

"And I thought that you and the Italian would be able to take out a couple of third-division hired thugs without blowing up half of the town square. But you know what thought did, as my old gran used to say."

"Too...friggin shay," says Duffy, struggling to his feet. "Shouldn't we be getting out of here?"

Robinson nods.

"Follow the white rabbit," he says, and he's off down the alleyway.

Duffy hobbles after him, keeping his knife in his hand.

"Like something out of a Hieronymus Bosch painting, isn't it?" says Walker, as a Clockwork Orange skinhead French-kisses an overweight transvestite. Then cracks a beer bottle over his head.

"If you're saying it's a shithole, well, you're right on the money," says Duffy.

And Patrick's really is a shithole, thinks Duffy. The building itself is fine. Oak doors. Marble bar. Silver chandeliers. And a very tasty old Wurlitzer jukebox. But the dregs of The City are drawn to Patrick's like a used condom down a toilet bowl.

"One of Dragan's most successful enterprises, though, I heard," says Walker. He sips a death-black espresso and turns his attention back to Duffy.

"Well, I think you'll find that this joint is owned by Mrs. Krystyna Kostic, actually. Dragan's wife."

"Yeah, yeah. Pull the other one, it plays Elvis songs."

Duffy pours the Budweiser down his throat without letting the bottle touch his lips. You never know what you might catch in Patrick's.

"So, who were the twats that wacked Giovanni and were ready to take me out? They didn't exactly look like The Frog Boys. They were good, too. Fast."

"Out-of-town contractors. Ex- CIB. Like you."

The cold sweat gripped Duffy like a cowl. Almost on cue, Barry Adamson's version of "The Man With The Golden Arm" started to play.

"I thought you might have recognised them," says Walker. "Maybe you worked with them during the Desert Wave? Are you sure they didn't look familiar?"

"No. Never seen them before in my life. A covert group like CIB had people coming and going all the time. Government policy, so you didn't get too loyal to each other and start up a mutiny when things went pear-shaped. You know that, colonel. You were there, too."

"Yes, I was, sergeant. And I also know that you owe me. You shouldn't need reminding of that. If I hadn't got you out of that prison cell, those mercenaries would have sliced you up and eaten you for lunch. Literally."

"I know, I know. So what do you want?"

"This is how I see it. Someone is trying to take out Dragan's gang. At first I thought that they were just after him, but now it looks like they're taking out everyone around him. To make Dragan as vulnerable as possible. And now Giovanni is worm meat, there aren't too many of your boys left."

"Maybe it's Rhino, maybe? A few of The Frog Boys attacked us last week."

"No. I think someone gave the info to Rhino, but there's someone else behind it. I think they were just sent to scare you off. You in particular."

"Yep, well, we're certainly dropping like flies. And those Hoodies are no use. So? Who?"

"Dunno. Maybe Ton Ton Philippe?"

"Come on, Walker. Don't talk cobblers. He's just a scare story that the Haitians made up. Isn't he? You don't believe all that stuff about zombie henchmen and werewolf bikers, do you?"

"Maybe yes, maybe no. But, remember, we saw some weird and horrible things back in the war, Duffy. Things that we couldn't explain. How do you think I got this?" He scratches the pentangle shaped scar on his neck. "Philippe's name keeps turning up wherever I look, these days. And as much as Dragan and you boys are a pain in the arse, this guy sounds worse. Much worse."

And then they hear the bang.

The building is ablaze. Flames lick the sky. Crackle. Roar. Outside Klub Zodiak, a handful of Hoodies shuffle around. Lost sheep. Arek is on his hands and knees, coughing his guts up.

Walker rushes over to one of the fire engines that pull up outside the building, and Duffy heads toward Arek

"What the fuck happened?" says Duffy.

He stands up. Wipes his mouth.

"Dragan happened. He cleared out the safe with a suitcase full of money. Took a plane out of The City," says Arek. "I drove him to the airport. He was rambling like a madman. Worse than usual. When I came back and opened the door…boom."

"So the house of cards really has fallen down, then?"

"Yep, looks that way."

Duffy hands Arek his hip flask. He stakes a swig.

"What about Krystyna?"

Arek shrugs.

"She went with him. Her and Lulu. But neither of them seemed too happy about it."

Walker strolls over to Duffy with a grin.

"Well, looks like you're out of work, Duffy."

Duffy shrugs. Takes a Mickey Mouse napkin from his pocket and blows his nose on it. Stuffs it back into his pocket.

"Not really," says Arek, "Here. From Krystyna."

He hands Duffy a large envelope. He takes out a wad of documents and a set of keys.

Duffy smirks.

"What is that?" says Walker.

"Payback," says Duffy and heads back towards Patrick's.

"Pop down to Patrick's for a drink later, boys. It's under new management."

"You arseholes could have killed me!"

Duffy is red-faced as he screams at Tennessee Bob and Davy Boy Ryan, who are sitting at the bar, grinning from ear to ear. "Nearly broke my bloody leg, too."

He half-heartedly drags a mop around Patrick's and then heads over to the jukebox. Presses a few buttons.

"We were just fucking with you, Duffy," says Bob, twirling his fedora on his index finger. "Had to make it look convincing to Walker and Dragan. And whoever else was watching. Had to put the shits up your old boss, eh?"

"And it worked, didn't it?" says Ryan, looking around the bar. "You got what you wanted."

Roy Orbison's "In Dreams" starts to play. Duffy walks behind the bar. Checks his inky black quiff in the mirror. Takes down a bottle of Dark Valentine and three glasses. Pours.

"You're a pair of twats," he says. They knock back the drinks. Duffy pours again.

"You going to redecorate this dump, then?" says Ryan.

"Eventually," says Duffy. "I'll just change the name for now. But I've got big plans, boys."

"You heard from that albino girl?" says Ryan.

"Yeah. She sent me a text. Her and Lulu have just got off the plane in Paris. Dragan hasn't."

Bob snorts.

"She doesn't waste much time, does she?" he says.

"All's well that ends well, then," says Ryan. They clink glasses and knock back more booze.

Outside the day is melting into night.

"Twilight time," says Duffy.

"Indeed," says Ryan.

Howlin' Wolf's "I Ain't Superstitious" kicks in as the front door creaks open.

A dishevelled figure shuffles in.

"Detective Dalton, what can I do you for?" says Duffy.

Bob and Ryan tense.

Dalton sniffs. Looks around the room.

"Under new management?" he growls.

Duffy nods.

"You seen Ice-Pick Mick McKinley?" he says.

"Not today, but I think he usually crawls in here at the end of the night."

Duffy holds up the bottle of booze.

"Want to have a drink and wait for him? It's on the house."

Dalton shuffles over and looks at the bottle.

"Why not? That strong stuff, is it? I fancy something with bite."

"Oh, yes," says Duffy. "It'll rip your heart out, this will."

Paul D. Brazill is the creator of the *Drunk on the Moon* series. He was born in England and now lives in Poland. He has had writing published in various magazines and anthologies, including The Mammoth Book of Best British Crime 8. He's also had two collections published: 13 Shots of Noir and Snapshots. His novella Guns of Brixton will be published in spring 2012. His blog is "You Would Say That, Wouldn't You?"

1942161R00122

Printed in Germany
by Amazon Distribution
GmbH, Leipzig